Tales of Zoalmont and

the Melancholy Fringe

"A young girl with her BB gun; a goopy-eyed boy in a dank basement; a muddy, drunk man hiding behind his father's freshly dug grave: these are just a few of the characters you'll meet—and become haunted by—in Mark Morelli's *Tales of Zoalmont and the Melancholy Fringe.* Arranged in the order in which they were written, between 1982 and 1993, these stories reveal much more than a young man earning chops as a fiction writer. The settings are vivid, conflicts concisely defined, and the themes are eternal: love, death, and the binding power of Italian cooking. Morelli also exhibits a finely tuned ear for dialogue—the stilted stammer of a father delivering "The Talk" to his son; the loaded Morse code of long-married couples; and the plaintive patter of whiskey drinkers. You will come to know, intimately, the keenly drawn denizens of Zoalmont, and you will carry them with you for a long, long time."

Kimberly Willardson Editor,
The Vincent Brothers Review
www.vincentbrothersreview.org

Tales of Zoalmont and the Melancholy Fringe

Stories: 1982-1993

Mark Morelli

BURTENSHAW
MEDIA

CUYAHOGA FALLS, OHIO

markmorelli.net
markemorelli@gmail.com

First Edition, February 2013, as *When My Life Was Fiction.*

Second Edition, August 2014

ISBN-13:
9798301757716
ISBN-10:
0692275274

BURTENSHAW
MEDIA

Burtenshaw Media • 830 Taylor Avenue • Cuyahoga Falls, OH 44221

Burtenshaw Media logo by
Abie McLaughlin Design & Illustration

Acknowledgments

Stories from this collection have appeared in the following publications:

"Rewind and Reflect" in *Changing Men*, Summer/Fall 1992

"Who Are We! (To Say What Stigmata With You)" in *FM Magazine*, April 1994

"Hunting Down the Burglar" in *Pig Iron Press*, 1991

"Afternoon Surprise" in *The Realist*, 1991

"Vikings," and "Armand Hates Tea" in *S.L.U.G.fest Ltd.*, 1991 and 1993. Judith Lindstedt later produced Mark Morelli's screen adaptation of "Armand Hates Tea" for television.

Dedication

For my mother, Nora, who bought me my first books and when she saw that I couldn't get enough, kept buying more.

For my father, Raymond, who helped me to see the stories that surrounded me every day.

For my wife, Lisa, who gave me the time to write.

For my children, Olivia and Julia, with whom I share this glimpse of my younger self. I hope you will be enriched by the stories that surround you, too.

Contents
Stories appear in the approximate order of when they were written.

Introduction

These are stories outside of the box.

I wrote most of them in the eighties, in my twenties. Back then, I indulged my curiosity for the world by writing stories. I was in college or just out. I was not yet married or just. The kids hadn't arrived yet. A computer was at first the size of a refrigerator, then it was just a typewriter that saved you time. The internet was around the corner. Ronald Reagan or George H.W. Bush was president. During this time, you didn't have to add "H.W." The vibrant generation that fought World War II was just retiring, still prominent lions in government, community and their families.

I wrote many stories, published a few, started a lot more than I finished. Our first child was born in 1993. The second in 1997. Finally, I threw all of the manuscripts into a box. In 2011, I opened it.

That's when these became stories outside the box. Or a magic lamp. Rub it, and out comes the past.

It was odd to read stories that I wrote but could not remember how they ended. The sentences were mine, but I didn't recognize them. That's when it occurred to me that someone else was the writer.

Isn't that what reading is all about, experiencing life through someone else's eyes? Even if that someone else is me?

Additional notes for the 2nd edition

My friend and tireless supporter, Ken Weiss, was among the first to read these stories. He pointed out that while these stories took place in very specific places and times, there is something about the world in these pages that is *otherly.* Ken called this mood and place "the melancholy fringe."

I immediately agreed that this describes what I felt and tried to describe in these stories, all of which began with a speck of autobiography and grew into fictional worlds of their own.

So I welcome you to the melancholy fringe, where the darkness isn't pitch, the sadness isn't depressing, and your front row seat out on the fringe gives you the perfect view to a time in small town America on the cusp of the digital era that happened not so long ago...but is gone forever.

Whippoorwill Sing

Not unlike, say, a war to end all wars, or capital punishment to deter murder, Annie pumped and fired three BBs into the back of the robin's blood-matted crown. Now it could rest easily, without pain. The bird was dead. She cried quietly. Nevertheless, she again pumped the gun, pointed the barrel tip as close as possible to the crown's warm blood without touching it and pulled the trigger.

It didn't fire.

She tried again, and again the BB had jammed in the barrel spring. Placing her hand over the tip of the barrel, she twisted the removable end. The spring unleashed and the pump released the BB into her palm.

Her hand stung, but her stomach ached more. The BB didn't cut flesh. She threw down the gun knowing the robin was dead anyway.

"Annie!" her father called. "Time for supper."

At supper, Annie's father told her not to leave her BB gun out in the yard. "That's all we need, honey. Because if that Wingley kid gets hold of that gun and blasts out their garage windows, his old man will have my head but good!"

He laughed and said to his wife, "I woulda loved to see Wingley's face when he saw all that broken glass!"

I don't know about that, Annie thought, remembering Mr. Wingley's face all sweaty and red.

"Have some potatoes, Annie," he told her. "Would you like a wing or a leg?"

Casper Wingley and Annie Hodge grew up together. At night they could both see the tips of each other's barns in the moon glow. They spent four years of misty mornings in warm and cold, sun and rain under the roadside bus shelter. Casper was the class troublemaker. Annie earned the best grades. Still, they were happy to play together. Their families got on well. In private, Mr. Hodge would end his nightly prayers thanking God that he sent Casper to the family one house down.

"Wingley's hand probably calluses so much from smackin' that boy's butt that he figures it really does hurt him more than it hurts the kid," he said with a laugh.

When they were in third grade, Annie and Casper found a dead finch on a path in the woods. Casper examined it closely.

"I wonder how it died," Annie said.

"Heart attack," Casper said matter-of-factly. He pulled out his Barlow knife and pointed the blade at the bird's head.

"Aw, are you gonna cut out its eyes, Casper? Don't do that.

"Relax. I'm gonna show you how he died of a heart attack." He carefully pried open the finch's beak, his own tongue curled in concentration

2

over his upper lip. "Okay, look inside here."

Annie watched closely, keeping her hands to her own side.

"That bird ain't got no tongue," Casper said, staring straight at the finch. "Least you can't see it." He looked at her like their teacher did. Twisting the blade, he opened the beak wider. "See, it died of a heart attack 'cause it swallowed its tongue and got so 'xasperated that its little heart couldn't take no more. Cat probably scared the hell out of it."

Casper put the finch in the pocket of his blue jean jacket. Later, he tied a piece of yarn around its neck and hung it from his brother's rearview mirror with all the other ornaments.

For her ninth birthday, Annie's father bought her a BB gun. "Now see here, honey," he warmly warned her. "We can't be having everyone around here playing with this gun. If that Casper Wingley wants to shoot it, you just tell him that your daddy said only you could touch it, okay?"

He took his daughter to the woods to practice shooting old tin cans. They were far enough into the woods for her untrained aim to be harmless. Occasionally, she hit a target and squealed happily. Mostly her shots would only rip at tree bark and poke holes in leaves. Then one day Casper Wingley ambled from a path onto the shooting range.

"Hi, Mr. Hodge. Hey, Annie! Wow! Where'd you get that thing?" He reached for the gun.

"Annie," Mr. Hodge said, his voice heavy with caution, "that's enough target shooting for today."

"Aw, let me fire that thing just once," Casper said. "Bam!" he blurted, mimicking a shot, picking off an imaginary something. Mr. Hodge took the gun from Annie.

"Why don't you kids go for a walk? Go play. And don't carve any trees!"

Casper and Annie ran down the path and quickly forgot the gun. They strayed off the path, climbing down a steep hollow and hopped on the stones by the side of a narrow, shallow creek. Casper walked in the ankle-deep water but Annie kept her new birthday sneakers dry.

"Wanna catch salamanders?" Before Annie could answer, he spotted it. "Jeez, lookit that!" Casper pointed to the baby sparrow, shivering, naked and featherless in the damp green undergrowth of an overhanging rock.

"Watch it, Casper. Mama birds can see for a mile and if they see you touching their babies they fly down and peck your eyes out."

"No sir, Annie. Anyway, no mama bird scares me." He picked up the startled suckling sparrow. "This thing better not pee or puke on me." He put the bird in his baseball cap.

They both stared at it. Casper concentrated intensely. Annie scrutinized the chilled sickly thing like a nurse. She looked above for the vengeful mother.

"Don't worry about no mama bird, Annie. Mother's dead. That's why she left the baby under this here rock instead of up in the nest." He curled his lip. "We gotta take care of it, now."

4

The bird was deathly sick, drained of color, fleshy. With a wooden match from his pocket, Casper probed it like a TV doctor. "Since the mama's dead, and this thing looks mostly dead himself, ya know what we're gonna have to do, don't you Annie?"

She shook her head.

"We're gonna have to put it outta its misery. For its own damn good, it's what we gotta do."

"Kill it?" Annie asked.

"Have to," he said, not looking at her. "Ain't got no choice."

He poured the sparrow from his cap onto a mossy slab. Annie watched closely. He picked up a boulder.

"Wash this in the creek," he told Annie as he tossed his cap to her. "Don't want no infection." She turned, stooped and dunked the cap into the creek. The sound of a shrill squeak, a peep that needled the air then instantly fell silent, made her spin abruptly back to Casper. She watched the stone roll sideways enough to see the painfully expanded jaws of the bird, eyes ready to explode, its insides gushing out.

"God, Casper! How do you really know that the mama is dead!

Casper was offended. "I know one thing's for sure. Some mama bird sure as hell ain't gonna leave no baby bird out here on a rock where anything could get to it and kill it. Mama's dead, Annie. That's all there is to it."

"Okay," Annie said. "I guess so."

They went searching for salamanders.

After Casper snuck off with Annie's BB gun he explained that he went "temporary crazy" and shot out his father's garage windows. Annie chased him down but he kept shooting out the windows even though Annie tried to yank the gun out of his hands. He wouldn't let up. He even offered her the last unshattered window, but she couldn't do it. But throughout the shooting spree, she laughed and jumped and squealed. She loved it.

After the garage attack, Mr. Wingley raised a few more calluses and Mr. Hodge ordered Annie to never let the gun leave the backyard and to never allow Casper near it. Casper's window sniping was the last straw. The next to last straw occurred the day before. Casper and Annie had been shooting soda and beer cans at the opening near the pond.

Ping.

Ping.

Casper was quite the deadeye. Day after day he came to monopolize Annie's gun. She didn't mind. She even cheered him on.

While shooting that day, he stopped right in the middle of a fast, steady volley of dead accurate shots. He turned to Annie and with an intense seriousness, shushed her.

"I can't believe this, man," he whispered. "I can see a whippoorwill sittin' on them leaves over there."

Annie squinted but saw nothing but leaves. She knew whippoorwills were hard to see. Her father told her they blended in with their surroundings.

"I love how them whippoorwills sing," Casper said softly, tugging the beak of his cap. Tongue curled, he slowly cocked Annie's gun. She still could not see the bird. Casper fired.

Suddenly, she could see the bird. It came alive! Fluttering strenuously, it hovered a few feet above the ground. Rising and falling with jerks, the bird kicked up colorful leaves.

"You got it!" Annie shouted excitedly while Casper struck a gallant Minuteman's pose. But he quickly abandoned his glory and set himself once again to duty.

"We gotta help that bird," he said. "We gotta do something.

"Yeah," Annie said. "We can't just let it suffer."

Casper ran up to the struggling whippoorwill. Annie followed.

"We gotta put this thing outta its misery," he said. He threw his head back and whistled a sound. "That's a tribute to the whippoorwill," he said, untying a shoe and removing a shoestring. He tied it around the sputtering whippoorwill's neck and swung the shoestring like a lasso. He screeched like a cowboy then released the shoestring into the air. For half a second, Annie thought the bird would fly away like a kite.

It splashed into the pond.

"Burial at sea," Casper said, saluting the bird like the men she saw at Memorial Day parades.

They walked home, passing the big oak "love" tree, carved with the names and initials of boyfriends and girlfriends. Casper was too short to reach any substantial open space, so with his pen knife he scratched his and Annie's names on another a small peach tree that Mr. Wingley had planted next to the old oak.

"'Member when that thing was just a sapling," he said, finishing their names.

"Yeah, barely. We were so little." Casper's name reached almost a full circle around the trunk, the C touching the R.

"Well, now it's a brand new name tree," he said.

Later that day, Casper's father saw the young tree his son carved up for friendship.

"What did your Dad say to you?" Annie asked the next day.

"He got real mad 'cause we didn't use the regular love tree."

"Yeah?"

"Yeah, but heck, I told him we weren't in love or anything."

"'Course we're not!" Annie said.

"But he still give me hell for carving up the peach tree."

"Did he give you a beating?"

"Nah, he just give me hell," Casper said, grabbing Annie's BB gun. "C'mon, let's go over to my house."

Since Casper was grounded for shooting out the garage windows, Annie played by herself in the backyard. She played with cards in the sandbox, rode her bike, swung on the tire, and was bored. She picked up her BB gun and took some pot shots at random birds. To be fair, she promised herself not to aim near her mother's bird sanctuary. For an hour, she snuck up as close as she could, and just when she couldn't hold her laughter anymore, she pulled the trigger and the bird would flap away frightened but untouched.

Bird after bird, BB after BB...the BB would be lost in the grass and the bird lost in the sky. She never had so much fun alone.

So she rolled, perched on her elbows, aimed and fired. And instead of the robin flying away, it fell to its side, wings flapping in pain and panic.

Annie's face twisted, confused and surprised and not totally sure of what was happening. Her neck thickened with tension.

"Gotta get it out of its misery," she said to herself.

It was close to supper, but she knew she could not go in to eat with that robin hopping and suffering, flying high as a basketball hoop then banging down on its beak. God, she thought, it might get a heart attack and swallow its tongue if the cat comes around.

Tilting the barrel, she heard three BBs rolling.

Occupant Mail

"Jeezus!"

Loudon's toe caught the jagged ridge of the disheveled sidewalk that led to the front door of the last house on his water meter-reading route. His nostrils could almost lick the peeling grayness of its smell. No doubt about it, this was the house. He had been warned. He double-checked the meter readings ledger to make sure this was his last stop in the notebook.

They don't use much water here, he thought, reading the past few years' numbers. Minimum amount always. He sniffed. Must be an old lady and her goddam harem of cats.

Above the typewritten name and address of this final house in the notebook the previous meter man had written in pencil, THE CAR DOOR KID!!!

He touched the dust on her mailbox. It left a clear fingerprint. He lurched as two toads bailed off the paint-chipped porch. His nose quivered at the smell of, what was it, cigarettes and sour milk and cat piss? He gagged, remembering yesterday's reek, which was even less offensive than this.

Yesterday he had knocked on an old woman's door and though he could see the tip of her head above a chair through the screen door, she would not answer. A television lit the room. He called to her but she didn't stir. He hated it when people ignored him when he could plainly see that they were home. But she wouldn't move. Five clotted-eyed cats scampered to the door crying and clawing the screen. Their onrush unsettled the odor and blew it Loudon's way.

The police arrived. Loudon answered their questions.

"If someone would just put these old people on some kind of mailing list then at least their goddam mailboxes would fill up and then the mailman would at least know something was wrong!"

"Get off your soapbox, kid," the cop replied. "This old lady must have been ninety at least. She couldn't have been saved by a mailman."

"That's not what I mean," said Loudon. "It's so easy for you to say, but I had to swim through that shitty air to read her goddam water meter. I'd of liked to see you try to hold your breath for that long. That's all I know, chief, that's all I know."

"People gotta die, buddy," the cop said, writing in his notebook. "Don't get too excited about it. Drink some water or something."

"Hey, I'm not getting excited about it. I ain't no idiot. I know people gotta die. And I also know that if people gotta go walking in other people's houses to read other people's water meters so that the city can charge them so they can have money to pay brave cops like you, then meter readers shouldn't have to walk through houses that smell like death. That's all I'm saying."

"Yep," the cop chuckled. "There oughta be a law. Now get off your soapbox, kid."

Loudon looked in the mailbox, something he wasn't supposed to do, but the day after he found the dead lady, he felt like he had earned the right. Especially because he had a bad feeling about this place, too. He sort of expected to see mail addressed to THE CAR DOOR KID. But there was nothing in the mailbox.

Through the screen door there she was. Another old lady. Another too loud television. To his relief, Loudon could see she was rocking slightly in her chair.

He twisted his nose at the offending odor, the reek of old waste in mildewy carpet. He closed his eyes. This was someone's daily life.

"Hi," he said, tapping lightly on the door. "I'm here to read your water meter."

She kept rocking and watched TV. Loudon thought he heard a scratchy growl.

He knocked a little louder. "Uh, hello? I'm here...to read...your water meter!"

The woman was oblivious to him and to the phlegmatic howl from the back of the house behind some door.

This sucks," he grumbled, spitting on the porch. "Hey, 'scuse me there, but I'm the water meter guy!"

He pounded on the door.

The woman sat in her rocker and Loudon watched her laugh through an ashtray full of smoldering smoke.

She leaned on her walker and reached for the pack of Philip Morris cigarettes on the coffee table. With a slow, unsteady thumb, she scratched a flame from the old butane lighter and sucked a puff. She exhaled, turned her head and saw Loudon at the door. She held up one finger and croaked, "Wait a second."

"Jeezus," Loudon grumbled, looking away to the bright street. This house was Kansas. The rest of the street, Oz. No sir, there is no place like this home. Another toad leapt from the porch, kicking a fleck of paint on his boot. The woman swung from her chair to the walker and slowly plucked at the distance of her faded rosy carpet. When she finally got to the door, she noticed Loudon's disdainful scowl.

"Smell like pee-pee here, huh? Been here long? Whatcha need, honey?"

"I'm here to read your water meter."

"Well, my hearin' aid fades in and out all the time. Sorry if I kept ya."

Stepping inside, Loudon heard a distant trumpet of wheezing and a hoarse yodel.

"New on the job, sonny?"

"Uh, yeah. Yes. First time for me. Which way to your basement?"

"Now let me see here," she said, lighting another Philip Morris while the other burned in the ashtray. "You look like somebody's boy. Whose boy are you? Who's your dad, honey?"

"Ma'am?"

He hated this. He hated when people tried to guess his family because the only ones who ever played that game had the smelliest houses.

"You a Pedunzo?"

"Huh?"

"You Alfie Pedunzo's boy?"

"No, ma'am, I ain't. I don't even know him."

"You don't know Alfie Pedunzo? Lord, he works down at the water department. Same as you. And you don't know him? Why, he's the one what put my water meter in."

Loudon would've sighed but that meant he'd have to take a deep breath.

"Mrreeebbrbrbrl!"

Loudon looked in the noise's direction.

"Well, whose boy are ya then?"

He didn't know any Pedunzo at the water department.

"I don't think you know my father," he said.

"You related to the McVays?" Lord, you look like you could be Josie McVay's baby. You sure have grown."

"Is this the basement door?"

"Yup-a-rooni," she said, frantically clopping behind him on her walker, following Loudon into the kitchen. "It sure does smell like pee-pee in here sometime. That's my cats."

Loudon scanned the kitchen. No magazines, no coupon books, no newspapers. No junk mail that could fill up her mailbox. Nothing but empty cat food cans and a centipede on the windowsill. Like it or not, he had to go to the cellar to read the meter, and in a house like this, that could mean some hideous treasures below. He reached for what he thought was the cellar door and heard a flat pounding of feet on soggy carpeted stairs. The door flung open toward Loudon.

"Waah!"

Cats and kittens swarmed at his feet – one blind, one bald with sores, all with matted fur, followed by an old slow toothless dachshund with its tongue hanging out on one side heartily trotting behind.

The scabby-faced, goopy-eyed boy stood behind the dog at the foot of the steps. Boy? Young man? It was hard to tell. He looked about twenty, but was small and reed thin. The boy's tongue flicked at his brown, stubby teeth and his palsied hands flapped rapidly. He excitedly wiggled his eyebrows and Loudon noticed a thick, round scar in the middle of his forehead, surely never to heal from all the finger picking done to it. The boy's face screwed into a sneezy wince, and he blinked in pee-pants excitement.

"Hewwoh," The boy's lips danced and he happily coughed.

Loudon was stunned into fear. He was not prepared to be cool, drowning in the stench of unkept animals and betrayed by the old woman, whose three burning cigarettes formed the smoky curtains of a spooky dungeon. Against his better, normal judgment, he breathed deeply.

"Cellar door's over here honey," the old woman said as she waved away the animals with a few flicks of her butane lighter.

He followed her finger. The boy followed Loudon with twisted steps, keeping a tense distance. Loudon watched nervously from the corner of his eye. Then he stepped on the blind cat.

"Mikey, you bring these animals back to your room, understand!" The boy – Mikey – stared at Loudon and kept two paces behind him, flapping his contorted arms.

Loudon gasped.

"Gotta flashlight honey?" the old woman asked and Loudon noticed her eyes staring at something else, something blank.

"Uh, yes. Yes I do."

"Yus," Mikey repeated with a grunt.

Loudon edged his way down the dark basement stairwell. Mikey followed. The boy tugged on a cord that lit a solitary bulb. The old woman on the step behind Mikey accidentally touched her hot cigarette into the boy's back.

The boy howled and Loudon cringed. Then the old woman kissed the boys back to make it feel better.

Loudon groaned softly.

"Try to keep my bill down honey," she said pleasantly. "You know where the meter's at? Course you don't. Over there by them old bricks."

He shined his flashlight into the dark corners of the ceiling and floor, checking for spider webs, rats and snakes. He smelled the dripping water he could hear. His stomach shifted when the boy cleared his gummy throat.

"My bill shouldn't be too high," she shouted. "Cause I don't always flush. Well, I flush, but not when it's just pee-pee. Only number two. But that's all. Mike flushes all the cause he thinks it's a game. Sometimes he flushes when he don't go at all. Sometimes he goes and don't even flush it down."

Loudon shined his flashlight from beam to beam, from brick to brick. He found the old water meter. Alfie Pendunzo must have installed it thirty years before. He jotted down the meter numbers, barely changed since the last time. The bare minimum amount of water had been used. Why had he even bothered?

He plodded heavily on the steps to frighten away Mikey. His boot slammed down on a rotten step, the wood collapsed and Loudon banged his knee on the next step up. Pain ricocheted from bone to bone and Loudon bit his lips.

The boy squealed, flapping his hands and banging his knees together. In his excitement he must have been picking at his scar for a trickle of blood ran down over his nose, a red Cycloptic tear.

17

"Are mah babies hungry?" the old woman said to the flotilla of infected cats. She filled up the stained plastic bowl with very hard cat food.

This has gotta stop, Loudon thought, straining to remember any kind of mail in the house. If the Car Door Kid dies, at least the woman could use a phone or something. Was there a phone? And if one of the animals die, then the Car Door Kid will probably wrap it up as a gift and give it to the old lady, and at least she would throw it in the trash. But if the old lady goes, no one would know, and the kid's throat is so glucky that his crying wouldn't be heard out in the street and it would be water reading meter time again...

"This sucks," he said and flung the cigarette down to the basement floor where it doused immediately in a pool of standing water. Mikey giggled through the brown stubs of ravaged enamel. Loudon got angry..

"Hey," Loudon said, startling her. "Thanks. I'm done."

"Oh! Forgot you was here. Well, honey, how much did I use?" She reached for her pack of cigarettes when she remembered she had one already lit in her other hand.

"Same as ever," Loudon said. "Do you get a newspaper, ma'am?"

"Don't read the papers," she said, her eyes spinning. Sucking at the cigarette, she opened a cupboard. I read what's on some of these cans. Vegetables. Sugar. All that stuff."

Mikey sneezed.

The blind cat bumped into a wall and Loudon noticed that its whiskers were gone. The boy touched the blood from his scab and Loudon looked away, afraid he would feel compelled to ask how the boy got the scar, afraid of the answer. He had to get out.

"I used to get TV Guides from the Books on Wheels lady. She used to come and give me TV Guides. But they were always so old I never knew what was on TV. So I told her to go away. Did you watch TV last night?"

"No, ma'am." Loudon moved to leave.

"You somebody's boy?" she asked. Mikey continued to touch his forehead.

"You don't get a newspaper here?" Loudon asked again. Something moved in the cat food dish. He jumped when the Car Door Kid touched his shoulder. The old woman scratched at something brown on her neck and Loudon noticed she was slightly cross-eyed. A kitten noticed the wriggling centipede and pounced. The boy squealed with the joy of touching the meter man and jumped back to touch himself. Loudon's flashlight dropped from his jacket pocket and shattered.

The throat-flushing squeal from the Car Door Kid was the convenient answer to Loudon's worrisome prayer. Perhaps the mailman delivering occupant mail would hear the boy after the boy's loud wailing of sadness and hunger and rescue him.

Loudon closed the water meter ledger and stepped out of the house. A toad leapt from the broken step. Startled, Loudon gasped, but the air was fresh. He walked off into the sunshine.

The Fever of Change

"Auntie Phyl!" Russell sprinted down the path. "Watch me climb the tree fort!"

Phyl's throat tightened watching Russell spring down the uneven path. She restrained herself from bidding him to be careful. So many times she vowed not to become an overprotective adult like her sister. Just because she was named for her grandmother didn't mean she had to worry like an old lady.

So often her mother and sister playfully, probably enviously, jabbed at Phyl's patience by ridiculing her ideas, warning her that after she put those college books away, her day would come. She would not become what she now despised. She promised to remain the eternal ragamuffin. She loved the word ragamuffin.

But now she felt worried for the first time. Why? Because Russell was running? That's stupid. Ten-year-old boys run. Jump. Fall down. That's the beauty of uninhibited childhood. Why should she interfere just because she was losing hers?

No, she hadn't lost it.

She loved running, jumping, falling down, crying. If the child's sock falls down, let it stay down. Children are supposed to be disheveled because life is disheveled. When adults try to artificially primp children's natural dishevelment, they destroy imagination. And without imagination, life is not worth living.

Auntie Phyl would not have a life without wide-eyed passion. So she shrugged, lifted her skirt and followed Russell down the muddy forest path.

"It's right here!" Russell said.

Auntie Phyl caught her breath, surprised that she broke out in a sweat so quickly. *I might be out of shape, but I'm still full of wonder.* She snatched Russell's Red Sox cap and perched it on her head.

"Hey, that's too small for you!"

She laughed, he didn't, and tossed him his cap back. She leaned against a birch tree, caught her breath, and took in the beauty of the woods. How wonderful to write a few lines now, capture with her pen the living verse that chirped and crawled around her. But, alas, her journal was back in the car.

Russell squealed with delight when they reached the tree house, old planks of floor and walls nailed to some branches seven feet above the ground. He picked up a loose, crumbled red clay brick from the dirt. "You know where this comes from, Auntie Phyl?"

"No, where?" She scooped gobs of mud from her loafers with a twig.

"They come from those old coke ovens over there."

Auntie Phyl turned toward the broken brick

ovens that lined both sides of what now looked like a weed-thickened canal but was once dry as a bone, lined with railroad tracks, where trains pulled up filled with coal to be dumped into the open air ovens that produced coke for making steel.

"They look like catacombs," she said, pausing for him to ask what catacombs are.

Russell hurled the broken brick toward the tree house. It caromed off the tree.

"Russell," Auntie Phyl said patiently, "What are you doing, honey?"

"Wrecking this place!"

She admired the little tree fort. She guessed that kids had spent days collecting discarded boards, mischievously play acting as spies to swipe the nails and hammer and saws. Then, she continued to imagine, they used their intuitive engineering skills – that have, since ancient times, attracted all children to playing with building blocks – created this make-believe crow's nest that hovered a few feet above the ground.

"Wreck it? Why?"

"It ain't my tree fort," Russell snarled as he grabbed the rope hanging from the floor above. He hoisted himself up by his bony arms.

Auntie Phyl studied her nephew. Did he expect her to join him in this destruction? Russell paid no attention to her. He yanked loose boards from the tree house floor. He tugged the wood and teetered at the edge, nearly falling over.

"Russell – stop that!"

He kept doing it.

"Russell! I'm shocked and disappointed with you! What are you doing!"

I'm tearing this damn thing down," he said, never looking up. Boards creaked, split and fell to the ground.

"Russell, stop!" Auntie Phil took a deep breath, then changed tactics. "Hey, Russ, you want me to climb up there with you?"

"No. You're too big." He tugged a rotted plank. It broke. He toppled backwards and nearly rolled off.

"Get down here right now. Russell! I mean it!"

He did not respond. He paused only to pull up his t-shirt and wipe his face. He glared at his aunt then spit in the opposite direction.

"This ain't my tree fort," he said again. "It's Michael's. And these are his dirty books."

With that, Russell kicked a bucket full of soggy, rotten apples and a few old Playboy magazines, which had been stuck together by rain and humidity. They fell like chunks of wood into the mud. As if by a divine hand, rotten apples rolled over the magazines, covering up faded photos of nipples and buttocks.

"Those apples were his ammo," Russell shouted. With each board torn up and thrown down, Russell had less room.

"Michael throws them apples at us if we come near here. Well, now I'm wrecking this place!"

Auntie Phyl wondered whether Russell was destroying it so that he could play in the woods without fear of being pummeled by apples – or if he just loved to destroy.

"Stop that! Destruction is wrong, Russell. Leave it alone. It belongs to Michael."

"Shut up! I'm tearing this thing down." He aimed an imaginary machine gun at his aunt and made spitty gunfire noises with his mouth.

"Russell! I don't believe this! You're acting like...like a demon possessed!"

He continued to tear up the tree fort. Auntie Phyl decided to storm the fort. Russell was too late in yanking the rope away from her grasp. She held on tight, the soles of her loafers slipping against the tree bark. She got a leg up onto the remaining platform.

"Get off!" Russell yelled. "There's no room!" He slapped at his aunt's leg like she was a pirate invading his ship.

She panted and scolded him through gritted teeth. "Stop it, Russell. Do you hear me!"

"You're not my mom!"

Auntie Phyl pulled herself up. Russell awkwardly punched at her leg but missed.

"Get outta here! Leave me alone! I hate you, Auntie Phyl. I can see your underwear!"

Russell started to cry. Sniffing and choking, he tried spitting on his aunt but instead dribbled all over his chin and shirt.

She was weakening. Her hands slid down the rope while her foot was still hooked to what remained of the tree hut floor. "Russell..." She gritted and strained while sliding nearly upside down. "Would you please...stop destroying...it's not...nice...to break things."

"You're not my mom!"

"Thank Christ," she said, finally swinging herself down to the ground. Her loafers sank into the mud.

"You better toss some apples up here to me in case Michael is sneaking around here someplace," Russell said, as if none of this had happened.

Auntie Phyl leaned silently against a tree, waiting for Russell to flush this ugly violence from his system. He shoved one more board over then climbed down the rope.

"Hey," he said to his aunt, "Wanna go catch tadpoles?"

"Yeah," she said sadly. "Okay."

He bolted ahead onto the path, then returned to his aunt's side.

"Take me to a movie tonight," he said softly, running a finger down the side of her wool skirt.

"I'm going back to school tonight, honey."

For a few moments he strolled slowly by her side. He reached for her hand, and then drew back.

"C'mon," he sang, jumping ahead of her and running backwards. "Let's catch some tadpoles. Race you to the pond!"

He ran ahead, but Auntie Phyl maintained her slow processional. When she reached the pond, Russell was squatting on the bank, cupping water in his hands.

"My God, Auntie Phyl, look at all them tadpoles! We shoulda taken that bucket from Michael's fort. I'm gonna go back and get it."

"No, you'd better not," Auntie Phyl said wearily.

Russell looked disappointed.

"Why? He ain't around. But, man oh man, is he sure gonna know it was me that dumped his bucket and broke his floor, won't he?" Russell smiled.

Auntie Phyl knelt to his side.

"You know something, Russ. I'm going to tell you something that you probably won't heed at this point in your life. Someday, you're going to think that doing something like tearing down Michael's tree house is kind of, well, stupid. Very unnecessary and unhealthy. Do you think you understand what I'm saying?"

"No, because me and Michael always get in fights and he's gonna know I broke his tree fort."

And he was also breaking her heart.

Blessed are the meek.

Boys will be boys.

"Russell – look! At the sunset. See how orange? Do you know what sailors in the olden days used to think when they saw an orange sky like that at night?"

"There's gonna be witches out tonight," Russell said, scattering the tadpoles with a splashing rock.

"I wouldn't doubt it," she said, gently grasping his hand to return to the house for dinner.

It Ain't Gonna Rain No More

Hunched over his smoldering campfire, Johnny Dee blew on the embers and poked them with a pinecone. At that rate, he would never cook on this fire. But he blew, and not only did the charred firewood glow, but also the entire sky lit up with a long blinding flash. A clap of thunder pickaxed the sky. Johnny Dee looked up to view the blossoming cloud belch up over the horizon above miles and miles of tree-filled hills.

"Well, I'll be damned. They actually did it."

Johnny Dee chuckled because the thought of this actually happening has always seemed so impossible. But there over yonder it bloomed. And he lamented the fact that he was alone. Whenever one of Johnny Dee's relatives died, the first thing to enter his mind was whether or not his dark blue funeral suit still fit or if it needed dry cleaning. In the same way, the first thought to pop into his mind upon viewing the white mushroom cloud punching up into the heavens was actually a craving for a cigarette after having quit three years before.

He chastised himself. "What the hell am I thinking about? A cigarette? I need a woman!" But he was alone. He cursed that fact. Sweat dripped rapidly from his brow. Wiping his face on his sleeve, he squinted at the hazy horizon where the gluttonous cloud gobbled up the sky. Whistling in awe, he shook his head, dazzled by the spectacle. But he had to laugh. It was because of all that political malarkey that he got away from it all in the first place. All those news bulletins and civil defense drills and stores closing and work being canceled...Johnny Dee just got fed up and went camping.

"Hey, I don't give a damn if you want to come or not," he told his buddies. "I'm just getting sick and damn tired of missing work. Goddam president this, goddam communists that. Hey, don't worry. If shit flies, I ain't gonna be missing out on any excitement just because I'm camping."

But Johnny Dee was missing out. Sure, he figured, he was just as vulnerable as his friends in town. But he never considered being alone. Stroking his bushy red beard, he forgot about having a smoke. He mused that these final moments were not only the last for him, but for everyone he knew. Then he wondered why he wasted time pondering. Yet what could he save his time for?

"What the hell kind of war is this?" he screeched, throwing up his arms in disgust up to the red sky. "Ain't nothing but a big can of Raid!"

He coughed and spat. Winds lashed his eyes. The air thickened. But he could not get out of his mind – and he didn't want to –– the faceless body of a naked woman. His mind flashed haphazardly with the blurring faces of the countless women he had ever wanted. His itchy skin turned pink. Johnny Dee's time ticked rapidly away, so he settled his fantasy on Cora, the elementary school teacher.

As he drove his truck past the school, Cora strolled behind the last exiting student. She walked to the truck, tossed her books in the back, then slithered in next to him. Then Johnny Dee drove them to the woods, to this very same spot where he pitched his tent and was watching the grand finale.

Cora peeled off her clothes and began to unbutton Jimmy's flannel work shirt with her teeth. How did she do that? She removed her glasses. Her hair was still tied back. The truck stereo blared. Johnny Dee bolted up at the sight of his mother and two sisters swinging their legs on the tailgate. One of them politely turned off the radio. No, no, no! They had to go! Because Cora the elementary school was taming his tattoo snake.

Johnny Dee gasped and fell backwards onto the steaming pine needles. Writhing and crying he watched oozing shapes of orange and purple turn into the dim light in the hallway near his bedroom door. He wrapped himself around the immaculate Cora for a rollicking loving to end all loving. His mother peeked in the door but quickly drew back. From his closet emerged Johnny Dee's two sisters in long scarlet robes heading for the shower. Johnny Dee squeezed his eyes shut then opened them to see the distant groves of trees all blazing. And he felt warm inside of Cora the elementary school teacher. Warm, then scalding white hot, till his spine melted away. Sucking his last gulp of molten air – and he knew it was his last – he bequeathed himself the will not to waste it coughing.

"Thank God it's finally done," he gasped, remembering then his desire for a cigarette.

Jimmy Hands

He got the name Jimmy Hands as a child in the Great Depression. The strong, wild boy attached himself with all his might and desperation to trees, to poles, to people and never let go. To poles and trees, no one seemed to mind. But when he clung to people, especially children, the people in the town of Zoalmont threatened Ophelia, his odd teenaged mother.

"We'll have the county take that child away," they said to her.

This frightened her. Jimmy was the only thing she had. There was no husband. She did not even know which boy was Jimmy's father.

Ophelia's own parents, who themselves were surprised by the arrival of Ophelia nearly twenty years after they were married, wanted nothing to do with their shameful wayward daughter. This didn't bother Ophelia for it differed little from how they had always treated her.

He got the name Jimmy Hands because of what the specialist taught him. The specialist was traveling by car across the country. He decided to stop in Zoalmont for the night. He stayed in the town's one hotel and ate his breakfast at the town's one restaurant. During the breakfast gossip he overheard talk of Ophelia and the bastard idiot child who clung to the very people who threatened to send him away.

"Don't want that child yanking at me," the specialist overheard one diner say.

"He clings to the flesh because he's a sin of the flesh," said another.

"He's bound to strangle an innocent child someday," said a third.

The specialist was a city man, political, fervent about helping the poor, especially during those hard times. He was intrigued by the stories he overheard and a few weeks later came back to town and taught the wretched unruly boy the most important thing Jimmy would ever learn.

Ophelia's parents never smiled or showed any love to one another, speaking their own old world language. Their almost beautiful (if she just combed this way or wore that dress) but confused daughter always tried too hard to find love and friendship. If she liked a boy, she did not bother with fine-laced language, the small talk that bought time. She just thrust herself forward, like a hostess offering free pie. She made love hard as any boy. Unlike a boy, she returned home with a face stung by tears.

When the specialist came and did his good work with Jimmy, Ophelia tried to thank him by wrapping her body around his. But the specialist waved Ophelia away. Your gratitude is enough, he said, furious with the town that enfeebled and punished her. You must never give your love away like that again, he said.

The specialist was the kindest person she would ever meet, a sad thing because she was only twenty-one and would live to be seventy. The specialist taught Jimmy one thing, to drop whatever he was doing, to unclench whoever or whatever he might be squeezing, and clasp his hands together obediently at the sound of the word "hands."

Ophelia grew bent and white-haired in Zoalmont with no husband. Her child became a man who continued to hang onto poles and trees and people, who did nothing but paw at things until someone said "hands." Then he would let go. Jimmy's grandparents considered him Ophelia's punishment from God and did not love or comfort either of them, but they did give them a room upstairs. When they died they left Jimmy and Ophelia even more alone but at least sheltered in the old house.

Weeds grew high in the yard. Neighbors complained. Ophelia tried to teach Jimmy Hands how to take care of the yard, but the brawny man with no sense would just push the shovel over and over in the same spot or roll in the weeds staring at the clouds. In the rare moments when she felt brave enough to think of the big picture of her life, she sunk into a deep, dark sadness. Ophelia trembled when she remembered the threat. "Be good, Jimmy, or the county will take you away," she said, more for her own sake than his.

On summer nights, the old woman and her no-longer-young son sat on their front porch in the cool shadows of a droopy willow tree. Jimmy Hands could not speak. But on these cool evenings, a more peaceful language hung in the air. The chirps and whistles of birds, the rusty squeak of the porch swing, the sound of children playing...as long as the children kept playing and left them alone.

During these moments the rare thoughts came. Ophelia would stare at Jimmy while he played with his finger or with the chain of the swing, with anything until he was told not to, and wonder if she was ever meant for greater things. Was Jimmy a blessing or a curse? If he was a curse, then was her wanton childhood worth the punishment? Would she avoid hell because of her earthly penance? And if he was a blessing...well, she couldn't see it. Though these thoughts were sad, thinking them comforted her, for otherwise her mind was filled with an even sadder thought, that Jimmy was just a useless animal. How bleak, to think that her life was spent caring for a beast.

Mercifully these thoughts never lasted long. Summertime in Zoalmont, like any little town, was alive with loud children and peeling bicycle tires and spraying gravel and it never took long for a few marauding children to shout "hands-Jimmy-hands!" as they rode by, aggravating Jimmy till he flapped his arms and honked like a goose.

Ophelia died on a summer day, in the bathroom, the door locked behind her. She would lay dead for two days before someone would hear yowling that came from Jimmy inside the house. He had pawed the door till his nails bled. The police burst into the bathroom to find an old woman whose gray, sullen skin was remarkably free of the wrinkles of laughter.

The paramedics wheeled out Ophelia and the police, who were not sure what to do, put a blanket around Jimmy. It took awhile, but somebody eventually suggested they find something for him to eat.

"There there, Jimmy Hands," said one policeman with a mustache who had known Jimmy all of his life. There-there was all he could think to say.

Jimmy Hands watched with fear and excitement as paramedics hoisted his mother into the ambulance. Neighbors in robes shuffled curiously to the sidewalk. Jimmy wept loudly then screamed in anger at the men taking his mother away. He slapped his own head and clawed at the two cops who tried to restrain him.

Hands-Jimmy-hands they said, out of breath.

Children gathered on their bikes in the front yard. A cop told them to get back. The young boys laughed.

"Hands, Jimmy!" said one kid. And Jimmy clasped his hands for just a second before raising them to his face.

"Hands," said another boy.

"Hands, Jimmy!" cried a third.

Jimmy covered his face, joined his fingers together, covered his ears, wiped his eyes, pushed away from the cops, over and over.

"Hands-Jimmy-hands!" said a tall boy with long bangs as he laughed and pointed.

Jimmy broke free and ran out into the street as the ambulance pulled out of the driveway. The police chased him. The children rode their bikes in a circle around Jimmy and the cops.

"Hands-Jimmy-hands!" they chanted.

Jimmy joined his hands then covered his ears. He called for his mother with a sound only she recognized.

One child rode too close and Jimmy grabbed him and held him tight. The boy shrieked and tried to break free. One cop panicked and drew his gun. The other cop said put the gun down and told everybody to step back and be calm.

"Shut up," this cop said. "Everybody shut up!"

"Hands," he said softly as he stepped toward Jimmy. His voice grew even quieter, more desperate. "Hands...hands...hands."

Things got quiet except for the sound of the cop repeating the word and the voice on the police radio telling them that county health officials were on their way.

Harold's Wedding Day

Lying quiet and still in Harold's brother's bed, I watched Harold's mother sit on the end of his bed and weep. The night before Harold's wedding day and she was bawling her brains out. I felt so squeamish and uncomfortable, and though I expertly faked sleep, they both knew I was awake, listening to every grieving word, every tear and choke. But they felt no shame. Harold's family was not what you'd call self-conscious. Tonight, Harold and his mother were naked with soul baring honesty. And now, they wanted me to be naked, too.

"What do you want me to do, Mama? I hate seeing you cry this way. It makes me wanna cry, too." But Harold did not cry. He might have been crying inside, but he never shed a tear that night before his wedding day. Oh, but Harold's mother cried. Her face twisted up in ugly mourning. In the shadows, she looked like a perverted horror movie clown. She quieted down. Her voice cracked. What the hell did she want from Harold?

"Do you want me to call off my whole marriage, Mama?" Harold asked calmly. Then he sighed. I felt snot running down my cheek. But I was so caught up in this drama that I dared not sniffle it back. It felt like a baby snake wiggling down my face, but I couldn't intrude on the privacy of Harold and his mother. I didn't dare move a hair. No bed squeaks. No sniffling. Not even fake snoring. Harold and his mother were in some weird tight bubble together and I didn't want to pop it.

The only reason I was a guest that night was simply because I downed too much Wild Turkey at the bachelor party. I knew I was not invited to sleep in Harold's brother's bed because I had somehow earned this private view of problems in Harold's family.

"Harold," his mother croaked, "Your girlfriend, she don't like me."

Harold's mother burst into sobs. "She just doesn't like me."Hell, there wasn't anybody in this town who liked her. The way she henpecked her husband, the first one, till he skipped town with the first scrotum-brained diner hag that was willing was testimony to that. The way she guilt strung her children so that they tagged along with the likes of just-passing-through carnival workers just to get out of her face – there was more proof. Good God, carnival guys could swoop into town each August counting on two sure things: Making money at the street fair and taking off with one of the girls from Harold's family just like hillbillies coming into town to fetch themselves a wife. And now look where we were that night, the night before Harold's wedding day, sitting in bed like it was a goddam slumber party. Four-thirty, I made out on the clock. Just two hours before the sunrise and the blistering, throbbing Wild Turkey headache that was about to kick open wide. I had drifted off till another damned freight train rolled by and then all of a sudden this crazy old lady stumbled into the bedroom and blubbered about not being liked. Hell, she could have confirmed that thirty years ago with one surprise visit to Willa's Beauty Parlor.

Just what right did she have, barging in on Harold's last leg of bachelor sleep? Why couldn't she just let him rest? Damn her, anyway, kicking out all of our best buddies. *Party's over, fellas, go on home now, get ready for the wedding. Let me have some time alone with Harold. A mother's got to have some special quiet time when her youngest son leaves home.*

We'd been having such a good time, too. I passed out on a pile of laundry. Damn her. And damn him for letting her ruin the party, kill the buzz. When I saw her break up the party, I told Harold that me and him should go get coffee at the truck stop. But he said no, he ought to stay home. Outside of that house, Harold was what I call a broodraiser, both a brooder and a hellraiser. He was the quietest wildass I ever met and I've known plenty all my life. We grew up together, twenty-four years on the same block, quit high school within a week of each other without even planning it. Harold wrecked cars, drank way too much, dealt a little pot here and there, played money games with hot car parts. But he never whooped up holy hell. Harold preferred manners and respect even if he was threatening to break somebody's arm. Too bad he wasn't Italian because he would've made good mafia man. He was like Don Corleone, always quiet, watching things, never missing a trick. He watched the world like a cat, real lazy-like, all the time fooling the mouse into feeling safe. But at home he dropped his guard. He relaxed. He listened to his mother.

"Well, Mama...I'll call off the wedding, then." Harold stood up, pulled on his boots. "That load of furniture I planned on running down to Georgia after the wedding, I'll just do that job now. That'll keep me outta town long enough for you to explain this whole thing away."

Harold and his mother both heard me gasp. Still I pretended to be sleeping. But I couldn't fool Harold.

"I know you're listening 'cause you ain't snoring"

I sat up.

"Harold, you're making a mistake." My voice was tired and raspy. It hurt from too many Marlboros and the bong.

"Maybe," Harold said. "Jenette is the best thing that's ever happened to me. But think about it. There's something that ain't right with her. You ever notice how cold and snippy she gets around Mama? Can you imagine how she might be around kids? You know I want to have lots of kids. And I wish they all could be the youngest, like me."

Harold was a man of few words. He made his decision, brushed his teeth, walked outside and fired up his truck. In that early morning, I could hear his eighteen wheels rolling and see his lights for a mile down the highway. He honked his horn as it dipped over the hill on the horizon.

Harold's mother and I did not budge from the bedroom for ten minutes. When the sun started coming through the blinds, she heaved a big sigh, lit one of my cigarettes and turned to me.

"I got Canadian bacon and blueberry muffins. You takin'?"

"Yeah, sure."

Harold's mother served me a fine breakfast. "Good coffee, ma'am."

"You don't gotta be polite to me." She refilled my cup. "Besides, I ain't in the mood for niceness. I got a hard task ahead of me today. And I mean hard. Over a hundred people expecting a wedding today. Now what do you suppose I am gonna tell that girl's family?"

I shrugged. Crazy old broad, I thought.

"Yeah, I figured as much," said Harold's mother. "Beats the hell outta me, too."

Dirty Windows

In the days when Zoalmont's railroad tracks rattled with trains, when bottles regularly toppled onto the floor, shaken from the shelves by one-block-away railroad traffic, Edgar Blackwell would hire some boy in town to clean the soot from the windows of his variety store. Back then, Edgar was too busy waiting on customers, cooking short order meals and selling train tickets to pay attention if there happened to be a kid loitering around the comic book rack.

But now Edgar Blackwell leaned still as a statue against his dusty wooden cash register. The windows were grimy, but not because of trains. He had plenty of time to clean them now, but he never bothered anymore. The grizzled old man squinted at twelve year old Bobby Packy at the comic book rack. Bobby flipped through the pages of Weird War comics, throwing his head back to toss the dirty yellow bangs from his eyes.

Bobby Packy heard no train whistles or rumblings from the great entanglement of rusting tracks across the street from the store. Nor could he hear loud arguments and backslapping gossip from the men drinking coffee and pop and eating sandwiches and pickles. He could not hear the squeaking wheels of luggage carts or the voices of rail travelers on their brief layovers asking for ice cold lemon blend drinks and local postcards.

Edward Blackwell could hear all these things.

The only thing Bobby Packy could hear was the heavy ticking of the old wall clock and Edgar Blackwell's wheezing.

Without even bothering to see if the old man was watching, Bobby slipped the Weird War comic book under his coat. But Edgar saw. He'd never averted his gaze from the boy. He watched, expected it to happen and it did.

"Don't think I didn't see you nick that book," he said. He wearily reached for his cane. "I'll tell you just once. Put it back and get out."

Bobby Packy cursed himself for getting caught. How could he be so stupid to let this geezer nab him? Bobby looked at Edgar Blackwell. What a slow and tired old man. An idea seized Bobby. As Edgar hobbled toward the comic book rack, Bobby stood firm.

"Are you kidding me? I ain't stole nothing!" Bob stomped down the stationery aisle. When he was out of Edgar's line of sight, he pulled the stolen comic book from under his coat and tucked it beneath a stack of notebooks.

"Get back here. I seen you steal the book. I'm not blind yet. Now don't be stupid. Get back here. Put the comic book back and get out, or else I'm calling Officer DiRocco."

Bobby returned to the comic book rack, stomping his sneakers defiantly on the floor. Edgar Blackwell leaned on his cane, face to face with the boy. The clock ticked away louder and tenser as it neared the top of the hour.

In the distance a train whistle blew. Edgar

heard it. Felt it inside. For a moment his eyes softened and the honk of the faraway train prompted him to reach for his pocket watch. His wrinkled brown fingers pulled at the frizzled fob. Then once again he stiffened his gaze upon the boy. Bobby Packy threw his chin in the air and his long blonde bangs flew from his eyes like startled pigeons.

"Open your coat!"

"I ain't done nothing!"

"You stole that book!" Edgar banged his cane on the hardwood floor, trying to sound thunderous. "Now open your coat and show me!"

"I ain't done nothing wrong!

Edgar Blackwell barred the door with his cane. "I'll close this store down before I let you out of here without you opening up that jacket of yours."

Bobby tried not to smile. He jammed his hands deeper into his coat pockets and bunched his shoulders together as if he truly were hiding something. They both looked up as someone tapped on the glass door.

"What's up?" It was Mike Horn, the guy who tended bar down the street at the American Legion hall. Mike spent a few years working for the railroad just like his father and grandfather but those jobs had been drying up since before he was born. The building that the American Legion occupied was once the B&O railroad passenger depot. The American Legion kept some of the old railroad artifacts in the club, which gave Mike Horn the opportunity to tell everybody how much he wished he could've carried on in the tradition of his father and grandfather. Truthfully, though, Mike Horn preferred tending bar to standing in front of a machine all day. Besides, he spent most of his time at the American Legion – his membership earned from two years in Vietnam – so why not get paid for it?

"You open, Edgar?" Mike Horn was puzzled at the face off between the old man and the boy. "I need cigars."

"I'm open, come on in."

Edgar unbarred the door, then spun around quickly, startling Bobby Packy. He pointed his cane at the boy's chest. "Don't you budge a hair. Mike, this boy here, I don't know who the hell he is...of course, for that matter, this town is so different anymore, I don't know who any of these kids are..."

"What's wrong?" Mike Horn said.

"Mike, we got a boy here who thinks he can take things without paying."

Mike Horn wanted only to buy two packs of cigars and get back to the bar. He had customers waiting and on top of that had just poured himself a coffee cup full of Jack Daniel's. He took a deep breath and sucked at a bothersome tooth.

"You Jim Packy's kid?" Mike said.

"Come on, Mike, you know who I am," Bobby said. "And you know I ain't no crook."

"He stole a comic book!" said Edgar Blackwell in a frustrated rage, pounding his cane down.

"Like hell I did, you crotchety old bastard!"

Mike Horn raised his hands like Moses. "Watch your mouth, Packy. Edgar, put down the cane."

"Mike, I don't need none of your help. It's my store," said Edgar.

"I know that," Mike Horn said. The train whistle blew again and without thinking Edgar knew it was turning Brackman's corner, just a minute outside of town. "I need a few packs of Swisher Sweets and I gotta get back to work."

"I'm outta here," said Bobby Packy, heading for the door.

Edgar Blackwell lifted his cane like a whip, frightening the boy into the sharp corner of a metal shelf storing dust-covered shaving supplies. Bobby's face went white with fear.

"Easy," Mike Horn said quietly to Edgar.

The old man cleared his throat and straightened his posture. He ran his slightly trembling fingers through his thin white hair.

"The boy stole property from me and won't give it back. I've had a thousand comic books stolen from me. In all these years I've caught you little sons o' bitches a hundred times. That's only a hundred out of a thousand. Bad percentage. If this was baseball, I'd be riding pine, wouldn't I, Mike?"

Edgar swung his cane slowly like an aging slugger reliving his one bottom-of-the-ninth tag. Mike Horn looked at the clock, knew he had to get back to work. He heard the loud, monstrous train chugging into town. He turned to Bobby Packy.

"Did you steal from Edgar?"

"He's crazy, Mike. Look at him. He's nuts." Edgar Blackwell lifted his cane. "Hit me – go ahead – hit me, old man, and I'll sue you!"

"Open up your jacket! I saw you steal the book. Mike, I saw him steal it. I swear I did. I won't call Officer DiRocco. I only want him to open up that jacket, put that book back, and stay out of my store."

"Packy, I gotta get back to the club. You heard Edgar. He won't call the cops."

Bobby Packy drew from all the movies he had ever seen and made up an Oscar-worthy expression of terror. Then he backed up a step, opened his jacket, look down in mock surprise at the fact that there was no comic book. He smirked at Edgar Blackwell then rolled his eyes at Mike Horn to say this old man was out of his mind.

"Hah!" Bobby Packy said as he flew out the door, kicking Edgar's cane out of his hand on the way. The boy spit on the sidewalk then let out a screeching Indian war whoop just as the freight train roared by, rocking on the rickety tracks, blasting its whistle.

"Hey!" Mike Horn called but quickly gave up on Bobby Packy. Edgar Blackwell stooped for his cane but Mike picked it up for him. "You all right, Edgar?"

Edgar shuffled toward his post by the old cash register.

"Forget it, Edgar. He's small potatoes."

Edgar didn't respond. He went directly to the cigar rack and grabbed two packages of Swisher Sweets.

"I gotta get back to the bar. Will you be okay, Edgar?"

"Do I owe you change?"

"I'll get it tomorrow."

Edgar Blackwell locked the door behind Mike Horn and flipped the sign over. CLOSED. He hunted through a shoebox of papers kept behind the old, now unused soda fountain. He looked through all the receipts and invoices for the old yellowed index card that was the only written recipe for the cheap lemon blend drink that his father had made that was the kids' most popular drink in town during the Depression. He couldn't find it. So he took a fresh long panatela from the shelf, lit it, then sat on a squeaky uneven stool. Puffing the cigar, he ran his fingers over the decades of gum stuck underneath the counter and gazed out the dirty windows. Nothing toppled from the shelves.

The Power to Move Mountains

Arnold Smith sat at his desk and stared out the window as old Boog Hemmetter hobbled down the sidewalk past the short rows of shops and businesses. The old man's gait was made crooked by age and his hardening superstition to not step on cracks.

The real estate office was quiet. The old oak filing cabinets had been in that same spot for nearly a century, outlasting four businesses. Julia Schultz, the secretary, sipped coffee and penciled in answers to a magazine quiz. Business was slow on a hot summer day. There was work to do but no hurry to get it done.

"Hard to believe you grew up in this town without knowing Boog's power," said Arnold Smith, a balding, middle-aged man with a red, boyish face, belly bursting at the buttons. Arnold Smith the real estate man was known in town for his fairness. Everyone told him he ought to be mayor, a testament to his reputable character.

"And if you don't mind me saying," Arnold said to Julia, "I've noticed you have quite a troublesome carbuncle there on your left thumb."

"Isn't it ugly?" Julia said, self-consciously covering it with the magazine.

"No wart is ever beautiful," said Arnold Smith.

"I got some wart medicine, but it just burns my skin. Maybe I'm putting it on wrong. Maybe I'm too sloppy."

"Yes," her boss said. "Or maybe it just doesn't work."

"Well, if that doesn't work, then I don't know what would. I hope it does, though. I don't want to go through life with this ugly thing on my thumb."

"Warts aren't permanent," Arnold said. "Besides, like I told you, there's Boog Hemmetter."

"You and your Boog Hemmetter stories."

"They're not just stories."

"They're not?"

"Nope."

"They're the truth?"

"All I'm saying is that they are more than just stories. Stories you read to children. Stories happen in faraway places. Stories have princes and dragons. There are no princes or dragons inside the old man limping down the sidewalk. Look at him."

"What's he doing?"

"Hopping over cracks."

Julia Schultz laughed.

"Arnold, are you telling me that Boog Hemmetter can touch this wart and it will magically disappear, just like that? Poof!" She waved her arms grandly.

"Why not?"

"You're serious, aren't you?"

"Yes, I am."

"He'll touch the wart and it will go away?"

"Yes."

"He just touches it and it vanishes?"

"Say it a thousand times, Julia, and I will answer a thousand times, yes."

Julia was at least twenty years younger than her boss, but Arnold Smith felt more like the child when he was around her. His awe and wonder brimmed in her presence, not because she inspired it, but perhaps because she was just all business, too serious for someone just twenty-two. It made Arnold Smith's day if he could make his secretary laugh.

"Well, I don't believe in such things."

"In what things?" Arnold asked.

"That he's some kind of Indian medicine man."

"Boog? He's not Indian at all. I think his parents were German. And he's not a medicine man. He just has the power to do that one thing. I'll call him in and show you."

"No!"

"Why not?"

"Don't you dare, Arnold. You'll embarrass me and that old man."

Arnold rapped on the window.

"Me?" Boog asked through the glass. Arnold waved him in. Boog Hemmetter nodded, wet his finger, slicked back the few remaining tufts of silver hair and entered the office.

"I can't believe you," Julia said. "Don't make fun of him."

"I'm not."

She quickly grabbed some folders and rushed to the typewriter.

"What are you doing?" he asked.

"I'm typing up some deeds."

"You can do that later."

"Don't embarrass me," she said, rolling the letterhead into the typewriter. "Don't be mean."

The bell tinkled above the door and Boog entered.

Arnold smiled. "Boog, how are you?"

"Oh, I'm fine, just fine."

"Everybody doing well by you, Boog?"

"Oh, sure. Can't complain."

"They're not giving you a hard time at the bank are they?"

"Oh no. We just like to rib each other, that's all."

"What brings you to town, Boog?"

"Post office," the old man said.

"Can I get you some coffee?"

"Sure!"

"Well sit down while I pour," Arnold said. "You don't take anything in it, right?"

"Not since the war," Boog laughed.

Forty years later, Boog still talked about sugar rationing.

"Boog, I was just telling Julia about how sad I am now that I got rid of my father's cabin out there in the Allegheny mountains. You remember that cabin?"

Julia smiled politely.

"I think I went hunting with him once or twice," said Boog.

"Yessir...the mountains," said Arnold. "Boog, speaking of mountains...remember telling us when we were boys about the power to move mountains? We can sell them, Boog, but we can't move them. We can slice a path or a tunnel through them. But we can't move them."

"Anyhow, Julia's heard stories about you and all, but she says she's not so sure about your power. Hard to believe, isn't it?"

"I've lost touch with the young folks," Boog said. "They're all moving out of town anyway. My kids are gone. Neighbor's kids, they're all gone. Are you gonna move away, too?"

Julia said yes. She would finish her secretarial studies at the community college within months and she had a cousin in Pittsburgh she could stay with till she got on her feet.

"I've been to some ball games there," Boog said. "It's a big city. Used to be smokey, just like around here, back when we had plants. No more jobs like that. No more jobs for brutes."

"But you still have the power, don't you?" Arnold Smith asked.

"You sure you wanna hear my story?" Boog raised his frosty eyebrows.

"Sure, she does," Arnold answered. "How else is she going to understand?"

"You sure?" Boog asked Julia.

Julia shrugged, still concealing her hand. "Why not."

So Boog told his story.

"When I was a boy in the twenties, there was revival tents that brought this town to life. No TVs and the big picture shows was in Youngstown and getting there before the freeways took some time. Anyhow, these caravans came rollin' into town just after the harvest, when all the work was done, sometimes just hours after the celebratin' calmed down. Lotsa fellas worked hard and drank just as hard, and a week later, they was saved by the preachers for the winter. Come spring they started to workin' hard again, then to drinkin' hard, and then get saved again, every harvest. I know some fellows got saved a dozen times. But, oh, them preachers, with their wild hair and bug eyes, how they'd scream. *Shame upon thee who has bowed to the god of John Barleycorn! Cleanse thy body, purify thy mind, for you have the power to move mountains!* That's the kind of preaching I heard all my life, but once when I was thirteen years old, them words just seared into me, and I heard them preachers like I never heard them before. Maybe I wasn't listenin' before that day, or maybe up to that time I was just plain too young, I don't know. But I do know that I was given the power on that day."

"Now I didn't do much with it for a few years. Just sorta let it soak inside me. Never even told anyone about it. Not even my mama and daddy. Well, sure enough, two years go by and I'm finally old enough to leave school. Lots of us quit school to work in them days. So I was workin' on

the Harn Brothers farm, luggin' milk cans,
pourin' grain into feed troughs, loadin' trucks,
when I start to think about them words. *You have
the power to move mountains.*"

"I was workin' with Quincy Powell. He's dead
now. And we're loadin' crates of eggs, me down
on the ground handing up and Quincy stackin' the
crates up on the flatbed. So for some reason, I
don't know why, I start tellin' Quincy about what
the preachers said about the power to move
mountains."

"Quincy said, *Why you tellin' me, I was there, too!* And I said to Quincy, *yeah, but you didn't get the power of the Lord.* And he says, *neither did you, Boog, so don't give me that look, coz I know you ain't got no powers from God.* Well, I just smiled and he says, *don't smile Boog, coz you ain't a preacher and you can't speak in tongues and you ain't got the power to lift them eggs without breaking half of 'em, let alone the power of the Lord.*"

Well, I had never felt more calm in my life when I handed him up some eggs and said, *I may not be a preacher, but I got other powers.* Well, he just took the eggs from me and was thinkin' a minute, not sure what to say, till he says, *all right, friend, why don't you tell me 'bout these...powers.* Then it was my turn to load eggs for awhile and figure out what to say. Finally, I said, *I'm not sure yet. And I ain't in a hurry to find out. All in the Lord's time.* Quincy just bust out laughin', tips a little, and a big crate of eggs slips from his hands and tears into a wart on his knuckle. Blood squirted from his hand. To this day I don't remember thinking much except that I reached up, touched the wound and said, *little mountain go away, tumble down into the valley of death.* Quincy, he showed me his wart the next day, pointing to his hand, and I says *ain't nothing there* and he says, *exactly.* To his dying day he says I cured him and from that day which is over sixty years ago I been helping folks out just like you, little girl."

"Very interesting story," said Julia. "Excuse

me for just a moment, Boog. Arnold, may I speak with you for a moment about this lease agreement?" She waved a folder. Arnold followed her to the back room.

"What's wrong?" Arnold asked.

"That was, well, interesting, but I don't feel right about playing with some old guy's mind. He seems like a nice old man."

"So?"

"So I don't want to play games with him."

"It's not a game, Julia. He'll rub it and the wart will go away."

"I don't know," she said, covering her hand. Arnold paced and looked in on Boog. "Coffee okay, Boog?"

"Yup." Boog saw Irv Holloway outside and waved. Irv raised his brows and lifted his chin – his version of a wave back.

"It just makes me feel kind of weird and nervous," Julia said.

Arnold Smith grew impatient. "Come on, this isn't Moses parting the Red Sea. What's the big deal? There won't be any talking clouds." Arnold marched back to his desk. Boog sipped coffee. Julia walked slowly from the back room to the front desk.

"Okay," she said, extending her hand to Boog, looking out the window. The old man examined the wart on her thumb like a jeweler inspecting a ring. He said words under his breath. Boog held the young woman's hand as if it were a sick bird and continued speaking to himself quietly.

"Mmm...the power...mmm...tumble tiny mountain....collapse into dust....the valley of death...mmm....mmm...mmm..."

He then lowered his head, opened his eyes and patted Julia on the wrist.

"There, young girl, it'll be gone tomorrow."

"It will?" Julia was surprised to feel a flicker of hope, even if only for a moment.

"Yes, it will." Boog smiled and finished his coffee in two big gulps. "And now, I have to go. I sweep out the American Legion every other day, clean their toilets. Keeps me busy. Bye now."

Outside, he waved to Arnold and Julia through the window. They watched him walk down the street, stepping over cracks, greeting familiar faces at the bank and hardware store.

"Has Boog ever cured you?" Julia asked Arnold.

"Probably."

"You're not sure?"

"I'm sure he probably did. He was the school janitor. We saw him everyday. I'm sure he cured me. He has the power to move mountains."

"This is just so fishy," she said.

"Think so?"

"It's just hard to swallow."

"I agree."

"Well, I don't get it then. In this dinky little town, why would Boog Hemmetter have the power to make this thing go away?"

Arnold shrugged.

"I'll tell you what," said Julia, "if my wart goes away, I'll give Boog Hemmetter ten bucks."

Arnold shook his head and smiled. He looked out the window. Boog Hemmetter was across the street sweeping the sidewalk in front of the American Legion building, looking up at the darkening sky.

"Looks like rain," said Julia. "We could use the rain."

Boog shook the dust from the broom. Old whiskey drinkers will be tramping that dust back in later that afternoon. Then Boog will sweep it back outside.

Arnold was just old enough to remember this town at war, when all those old afternoon whiskey drinkers were the sturdy young men, the brothers and uncles who fought the Germans and Japanese. Those were sad days, when some brothers and uncles never came home. But Arnold also remembered them as comforting days because everyone had some sort of faith. Telegrams announced sons who died on battlefields and news headlines reported the deaths of thousands. Enough blood spilled to fill a sea and yet there was faith. Though life hung in the lurch, suspended by a twine that continually unraveled, people silently agreed to believe in the same things. If the twine snapped, someone cushioned the fall.

Arnold Smith watched Boog Hemmetter reach out his hand to feel the first drops of rain. Arnold remembered the rain of his boyhood, when folks turned up their collars and ducked under awnings, the very same awning secured by rusty bolts to his own building. Rain became a spare moment to say hello, to catch up, to bless someone.

Arnold Smith knew that Boog and all the old-timers believed in the power to move mountains. And Arnold could see that Julia Schultz and her friends clenched their jaws defiantly in the face of such things that relied on faith, and instead, forged on with their lives with faith only in themselves and their own abilities, and God help you if that ran out, if only there was a God.

The Heroism of Gaetano Sferra

Gaetano Sferra went blind on the Pacific island of Saipan in 1944. He returned home to Zoalmont a war hero but did not tell a soul the truth that he lost his sight drinking tainted homemade gin. No one asked how it happened and when he made up stories of Japanese bombs that sprayed mists of chemicals in the faces of American boys, they shushed Gaetano, uncomfortable for themselves and for the boy who came home blind.

More than forty years later he sat on his front porch with the youngest of the Hatch children who lived down the street. Gaetano was showing Waldo Hatch how to relax.

"It is possible," he told Waldo, "to feel your hair grow if you know how to sit absolutely still."

He taught Waldo how to listen to rain.

Waldo had just turned ten. For the first time, Waldo Hatch stumbled upon a discovery of his own, this curious old blind man who lived alone three houses down. During the spring, Waldo approached neighbors to earn money mowing their lawns. It took only twenty minutes to mow old Gaetano Sferra's yard, but he would end up spending an hour and a half just talking to the man on his porch afterward. For great chunks of mornings and afternoons that entire summer, Waldo listened to Gaetano tell bit by bit the story of his life.

"And this is how it ends, Waldo, as we sit here on the porch. So far, knock on wood." Gaetano reached for the screen door. "Is this wood?" he asked. Waldo laughed appreciatively.

"I grew up in hard times, Waldo. Right here in this house. Times were harder than you can ever imagine. There was no cereal with sugar on top. Do you know what we ate for breakfast?" Waldo knew. He'd heard this before.

"No, what?" Waldo asked.

"Potatoes and onions and black coffee, even when we were little children. There was no TV. In fact, I've never seen television in my entire life. I hear it stinks, though." He held his nose, silly as a clown, and the boy laughed again.

"Then I went to war, came home blind. They made me grand marshal of all the town parades for a few years. Then Mama and Papa died and the years went by and now, here we are Waldo, sitting on the porch listening to the rain."

They sat peacefully for a few moments.

"Guess how many raindrops have fallen in the last minute," he asked the boy.

"A million at least."

"Close," Gaetano said. "A million and seven. No, make that eight. A million and eight. I think I counted one raindrop twice." He leaned back and sucked on his unlit pipe and waited till the boy giggled.

Gaetano enjoyed the boy's company. Too many people checked their emotions around him. They balked awkwardly in the middle of perfectly natural comments like "Nice to see you" or "See you later," afraid they would sadden Gaetano by reminding him that he was blind. The old man always wanted to laugh and say he didn't need anyone to remind him he was blind. Waldo Hatch did not yet know how to be embarrassed by Gaetano's blindness.

"Waldo!" cried Mrs. Hatch a few doors away. "Lunch in ten minutes!"

"Be right there!"

The boy tapped Gaetano softly on the shoulder.

"Gotta go, Guy. Oh, almost forgot, my mom said to ask you if you want to have lunch at our house today?"

"No thank you, Waldo. I'm not very hungry today."

"She said if you didn't want to come over that I should ask you if you wanted us to bring lunch on a plate to you. She's worried that you don't get the right nutrients."

Gaetano laughed. "Mothers worry so much." Waldo, before you go, would you make me a nice hot cup of tea in the microwave?"

"Sure."

"And Waldo?"

"Yes?"

"Why would I want to drink hot tea in the summertime?"

66

"Because it raises your body heat and that way the summer heat don't seem so hot?"

"Bravo."

Gaetano followed the sounds. The screen door squeaking open, whacking shut, water falling from the faucet to the cup, the microwave oven door opening, closing, the timer being set with beeps, then the minute-twenty of heating, which sounded like a tropical wind.

Gaetano was never a comfortable hero. He returned from the Pacific to a parade. They propped him up in a car and he waved to the noises of a couple hundred voices that rang bells in his head. The Zoalmont library named a reading room for him. Each Memorial Day, he marked the occasion in dark glasses with other veterans, his hand holding the elbow of a fellow veteran. He hated the sound of gunfire salutes.

All this because of that yokel boy Jimmy Lee Klinky.

It rained constantly that night in the Saipan jungle as two young Americans on guard duty leaned wearily on trees, their tired hands tensely gripping rifles.

"I still don't know where the hell we are," Jimmy Lee Klinky said, waving away mosquitoes. "You show me a map of the Pacific and I still couldn't find this goddam place."

"It sure isn't Ohio," Gaetano said.

"Ain't Kentucky, either."

The rest of the 105th Infantry sprawled out like wet green rags on the ground nearby, sleeping fitfully from bugs and nightmares – and worse – their dreams were taunted by mothers and pies, girlfriends and kisses. The two standing guard spat curses, talked big, but lit their cigarettes in cupped hands with shaky fingers. They did not talk about jungle traps, snake pits, beetles the size of Buster Brown shoes.

They spoke not of their enemy, wily gremlins hunkering in the thick green, invisible and magical and able to fly, with talons and razor beaks, with evil laughter that froze the blood. They did not speak of these things.

Gaetano tried to comfort himself by thinking of home. One year before, the night before he enlisted, his mother had burst into Sully's Tavern on Steel Street and smacked the glass of whiskey from his hand.

"Too young!" she cried while all the other drunks laughed. She clapped her hands to Gaetano's head. "Non sei un maleducato. La bottiglia e vuota. Piacere vieni a casa, caro figlio."

In the inky Saipan night, wings flapped and birds screamed, sounding like the shatter of glass on the floor of Sully's Tavern.

Don't be an idiot. The bottle is empty. Come home, son.

Gaetano's hands strangled his rifle. Mama, come now and slap this gun from my hand. Yank me from this island. Bring me home.

Gaetano and Jimmy Lee Klinky blew cigarette smoke at blood-hungry swarms of bugs. Rain patted the treetops, trickling down leaf by leaf to the sprout-tangled jungle floor. Birds squawked and whistled and hooted.

"I *hope* those are birds," Gaetano whispered to Jimmy Lee and God.

Sounds like a goddam amusement park," Jimmy Lee said. Something swung from a tree. Jimmy Lee was first to raise his rifle. It was a monkey.

"I'm going nuts! If I don't get my head blown off, I'll have me a heart attack!" Jimmy Lee pulled a clear bottle from his pack. "Got this from that Polack tail gunner before we landed. Boy from Looziana. Made it himself, he said. If this don't relax us, don't know what will."

"On guard duty?" Gaetano said.

"I need a goddam drink!" Jimmy Lee poked his knife into the cork. He noticed Guy. "You're shakin'. Look at you, Guy. You're shakin', man."

"What's new for today, Perkins?" Gaetano asked the mailman.

"Not much, Guy. Don't see any bills here."

Waldo brought out the tea.

"No news is what, Waldo?"

"Good news," said the boy. The men chuckled.

"So long, Guy," said the mailman.

"I better be going, too," said Waldo.

Gaetano wasn't feeling well. He did not want Waldo to leave.

"Waldo, did I ever tell you about the miracle of mail?"

"No," said Waldo, halting at the second step.

"Think of it. Let's say I have a sweetheart in Hawaii. Hey, why are you laughing?"

"You got a girlfriend in Hawaii?"

"I just might, Waldo. I don't think it's impossible, do you?"

"No," Waldo laughed.

"I didn't think so either," Gaetano said, pretending to be offended. "Anyway, let's say I write a love letter to my Hawaiian sweetheart. 'My love, I miss you so! I cannot bear another Ohio winter here alone while you sit so melancholy on the great sandy beach, your green eyes watching the mighty blue ocean, your tears deepening the sea, drop by drop.' Pretty sweet, mmm?"

Waldo agreed.

"And then I put my words into an envelope, drop it into a box on the street corner, and for the price of a twenty-five cent stamp, a man in a blue uniform – Perkins wears blue, right? – a man in a blue uniform will be my personal delivery boy. He'll pass my love letter along to other people in blue uniforms, in trucks and boats and airplanes, till finally, way over there in Hawaii, someone will drop it into my lady's mailbox. It's a miracle, don't you think, that so many people work so hard to bring my words of love to my lady. All the way to Hawaii? All for a quarter?"

"Never thought of it that way," the boy said.

"That's because you've never been in love. Or have you?"

"No way," Waldo said.

"There will be a day..."

"Never!"

"Oh yes." Waldo wagged his finger. "Oh yes."

"Well, maybe."

"Waldo, did you know that love is all around you at this very moment?"

"Where?"

"Listen."

"To the rain?"

"Listen."

"All I hear is rain. And that car."

"Listen, Waldo."

Waldo and Gaetano hushed.

"Oh...birds," said Waldo.

They pulled their chairs to the end of the porch.

"Listen," said Gaetano.

Above them, cardinals pitched woo back and forth from tree to tree. Gaetano smiled, baring his old, silver-filled teeth. He turned his head from left to right, listening to each bird calling from the two birch trees out front.

"Listen to them, Waldo. Listen to them sing. What is the boy cardinal singing, Waldo?"

"I don't know," the boy said, fascinated.

"Can't you hear him singing?"

"Yes."

"What's he singing, Waldo?"

"I don't know."

"He's singing 'Damn the rain! I'm in love! Come over to my tree! Come over to my tree!' That's what he's singing."

"And," Waldo added, "he's singing, 'I don't got a quarter to send you a letter coz I'm a bird and birds don't have any money."

"Yes, I heard it, too. And what's the girl cardinal singing, Waldo?"

"I don't know."

"Listen. Keep listening. What's she singing?"

"Ummm...she's singing, 'No, I'm the girl, why don't you come over to my tree.' That's what she's singing."

"Yes, I believe you're right," Gaetano said. They listened longer.

"Waldo, let's go out into the yard."

The boy extended his shoulder. Gaetano hooked his hand beneath it and they walked off the porch.

"Let's go under the tree so we won't get wet."

"I don't mind getting wet," Waldo said. Gaetano laughed.

"Oh that's right. I've forgotten there are still people who aren't afraid of rain."

Under the trees they listened intently, raindrops splashing off their squinting faces."

"I heard cardinals," Gaetano said. "And – let's see – a robin!"

"There's a nest," Waldo said.

"A nest? Have you ever seen the nest up close?"

"No."

"Oh, you must see the nest. Climb up and look at the nest. Tell me what you see."

Waldo hopped and grabbed a limb. Gaetano listened to branches creak as the boy hoisted himself up.

"Are you there yet?"

"Not yet," the boy answered.

"Keep climbing, son."

The boy's sneakers squeaked on the wet branches. He climbed to the nest.

"Look closely," Gaetano said.

"I am."

"No, get closer. People never get close enough to things. They think they do, but they're always a mile off. You've got to get your nose dirty, Waldo. Are you close now?"

"Yes."

"How's it look?"

"It's great."

"Are there any eggs?"

"No eggs. There's twisty ties like from bread bags. There's a rubber band, feathers and twigs, hair, paper, a little tiny bone, some yucky yarn..."

"Wonderful! Fantastic! Waldo, do you know what genius made that nest?"

"A bird is a genius?"

"With nothing but a beak, Waldo. No drills or hammers or nails or glue. Just a beak – genius!"

"Wow," Waldo said softly as he peered even closer into the nest. When he looked down again, Gaetano was crumpled in the wet grass.

Bark tore into Waldo's legs as he shimmied down the tree in a panic.

"Gaetano?"

"Give me a hand, son."

"Gaetano?"

"I'll be all right, Waldo. It's just slippery out here. Lead me to the porch and I'll finish my tea."

Waldo did as he was told. Gaetano sat slowly into his porch chair. The birdsong grew louder in his head.

"Waldo, is there a band practicing? A marching band? I believe I hear a tuba. And a bass drum. I hear a marching band, don't you?"

"I don't hear anything," Waldo said.

"Has St. Lucy's started band practice?" Gaetano asked.

"No, it can't be St. Lucy's coz we closed down last year. Mom's mad coz now I gotta take the bus to public school."

"I graduated from St. Lucy's," Gaetano said, the pain in his chest subsiding. "Remember me telling you that, Waldo?"

"The class of 1943," he said and Gaetano nodded. "And you played the slide trombone in the congo band."

"Combo. Do you remember the name of my combo?"

"I think so. The...Vienna...Walts."

"That's right and how was it–?"

"–It was spelled W-A-L-T-S. You said it was a joke."

Gaetano suddenly lifted his hand to shush the boy.

"There it is again. The band. Can't you hear the marching band, Waldo?"

Waldo tilted his head to hear better. He cupped his ear and closed his eyes, but he heard nothing but rain and cars and birds singing love songs to one another. He ignored his scraped legs and listened intently.

Gaetano had been blind for so long that he couldn't remember the faces of his youth. But at this moment Gaetano could see perfectly his parents. There was his father at middle age with that thin, unsmiling face, small dark eyes close together, a pointed nose that flared silently when he did not get his way, the stifled frown of a railroad man who spent his life shoved from one job to another, home for awhile, then gone west or south for two-week stretches, a man who did not know his wife and son, and figured little in their lives. And there was his mother, whose clenched jaw and stern brown eyes always melted into a smile and an encouraging wink, the soul of the household – its love, its hatred.

The last time Gaetano saw his mother was that night before he enlisted, when he was drunk in Sully's. He did not see her the next morning for she had remained in her room, praying that God look out for her only child, also praying generously for the souls of the war makers. All these years later, Gaetano wondered which of his parents he most resembled.

"Where's my tea? Gaetano asked softly.

"In front of you. Spoon is on the left."

"Thank you. Waldo?"

"Yes?"

"What do I look like?"

The boy waited a moment. The uneasiness in Gaetano's voice troubled Waldo. The boy learned to not answer questions immediately since he discovered the importance of words by listening to the blind man. Just months before, Waldo might have blurted his answer. *I dunno. Old I guess. White hair. I dunno. What do ya mean?*

Today Waldo painted his words. He spoke slowly.

"Your hair is snowy...like a mountain top. Your hands are like spiders that crawl on the table in front of you when you're trying to find things...a knife and fork and napkin...when you are making sure everything is in its place."

Waldo stopped and looked more closely at his old friend, who seemed to be thinking of something else.

"What do I look like?" Gaetano whispered.

The entire island was honeycombed with underground Japanese positions. Enemy machine gun nests could be anywhere. The Japanese attacked at night, bursting into camps, filling the air with screams and gunfire, then slipping back into the jungle, splintering the 105th Infantry. Gaetano saw some of the bravest men he knew panic and flee, swimming like maniacs toward the offshore reefs.

"Think Bob Hope's gonna come see us out here?" Jimmy Lee Klinky said.

Gaetano made himself laugh, lit another smoke. His hands did not shake as much as they wagged, a palsy of intense fear.

"I'm scared, too," said Jimmy. "I got a wife and a baby."

Gaetano looked at Jimmy. Whiskerless, he looked both babyfaced and fierce in the cigarette glow.

"You don't seem scared," Gaetano said.

"I'm scared shitless." He jammed his knife deeper into the cork and twisted. "What scares me most is not knowin' what's out there. In school books, war was like this army was in red and that army was in blue, lining up in a field, kneelin' down and shootin'. Here, a toucan might be a Jap and a Jap might be a toucan."

With a bottle and cork in his hands, a cigarette in his lips, Jimmy used the corner of his mouth to blow stray strands of his sweaty blond hair out of his eyes. They both jumped at a sudden, creaky noise in the darkness. Gaetano's eyes bulged in fear and he shook.

"Guy–Guy–you okay?" Jimmy whispered. Jimmy Lee Klinky gave the bottle to Gaetano. "You go first. Get yourself steady, brother." He put his face up close to Gaetano, like a cousin kissing his cheek. "It's okay. Toss some down. It'll take off the rough edges. Goddammit, I hate not knowin' what that noise is. Stay right here at this tree. I'm takin' a look. Maybe the moon'll give me some light. Maybe I'll see somethin'. I'll be just a second."

Gaetano was alone. He desperately gulped the bottle. It was nothing like the dry, tart wine from the neighborhood. It burned his throat, trickled like molten oil into his stomach. He doubled over and held his gut, like he had been stuck by a bayonet. His head spun and he dropped the bottle. Jimmy was there in a second, cradling Gaetano in terror and confusion. "What happened, Guy? Did they stick you?"

They both heard the rapid footsteps. At first it sounded like a pocket of rain falling from a heavy leaf. Then the pitter-patter grew louder, faster. Gaetano was sick from poisonous bad gin. But he was even sicker from the hot, empty fear of enemy footsteps in the crackling swordgrass. Jimmy Lee Klinky dropped Gaetano and fumbled for his rifle. Gaetano's vision blurred quickly but not before he saw in the moonlight the short young Japanese soldier tear through the campsite lobbing one then another grenade. Before any of them exploded, Gaetano Sferra's vision went black.

"Gaetano! Are you all right?"
Gaetano did not answer.
"It's me – Waldo!"
The old man's fingers crawled up and down the row of buttons on his flannel shirt. He did not want to frighten the boy. But Waldo knew Gaetano was in great pain. The old man trembled.
"I'm gonna call my mom."
"No, Waldo. I'm fine."

Waldo wanted to believe but he was afraid.

"Are you sure?"

"Yes."

Waldo was kind to Gaetano. He planted tomatoes in the backyard, mowed the lawn, made trips to the post office and pharmacy for him. Waldo was a friend. Friends should not be lied to. Gaetano did not want Waldo to remember him as one who withheld truth from a friend. But there were many truths Gaetano held inside. Which one could he tell the boy?

"Is it raining? I'm wet and cold."

"You're on the porch." Just then one of Waldo's friends ran by.

"Hey, Waldo!"

"Hey, Mike." Waldo kept a steady eye on Gaetano.

"Wanna go play football in Nickleby's lot?"

"Can't. I gotta go eat."

"Come on, Waldo, we need another guy."

Gaetano now felt sick and weak and feeble-minded. Was Death pulling him away? Death did not matter yet. Life still did. Gaetano searched his drifting mind to discover how he could still make a good mark in his life, to deserve to be feted in all those parades.

"Are you going to lunch, Waldo?" Gaetano whispered.

"No. I'm not hungry."

"Good...you shouldn't eat if you're not hungry. Go play." The old man groaned and winced.

"Gaetano...?"

"You coming?" asked Mike, riding impatient circles on his bike on the street.

"Can't, Mike."

Waldo sensed wrongness somewhere.

"Mom says you should come to lunch with us," Waldo said.

"No, I'll just finish my tea." Gaetano weakly lifted his hand toward the table.

"I'll hand it to you."

"No, I'll get it."

Gaetano sat up slowly and reached. His hands came nowhere near the cup.

"Damn it. Where is it? Where is it, Waldo?"

"Here, Gaetano." Tears filled Waldo's eyes. He handed Gaetano the teacup.

Gaetano sipped. "Waldo? Are you still here?"

"Yes," the boy said, placing his hand in Gaetano's. Mike sped away on his bike. They sat quietly for a moment.

"Waldo?"

"Yes?"

"You enjoyed my stories?"

"Yes."

Gaetano's spirit returned. The pain went away. The dizziness was gone.

"They were good, good times. Of course, these will be the good times for you, see? When I was a boy, all the old men, some were so old that they were in the Civil War, said their days were the good old days."

"Your days sounded good."

"Well, maybe good is not the right word. I don't know what the right word would be. I grew up in a world run by insane men so hungry for power that they sent millions of us to die on battlefields and in ovens."

"But you fought the bad guys. You were a war hero."

He squeezed the boy's hand. "Not a hero," he said so softly that Waldo couldn't understand. Sudden pain stabbed Gaetano. He gritted his teeth and groaned.

"Gaetano?"

"Sshh. Waldo, come here."

"Mom!" Waldo pulled away.

"Ssh-sshh-sshh. Come here, Waldo."

"Mom! Gaetano's sick!"

Gaetano reached for Waldo's hand, grabbing at air. Waldo ran back to him and placed his small soft hand in the old man's.

"Is that St. Lucy's band?" Gaetano asked again.

Waldo sniffed back tears.

"Do you hear it, Waldo?"

"No."

"You don't hear it?"

Waldo gulped.

"Come closer. Listen...listen, ragazzo. Up and down this street, it was all Italians. When I was a boy like you, in this house, on this porch, all the neighbors....the Booglebeenis and the Cockameemis and the Raviolis...."

Gaetano burst into laughter. Waldo tried to join in but he really just wanted to scream for his mother. Gaetano's laughter sputtered into coughs.

"That's what we were around here. A bunch of spaghetti-benders. And now, I'm the last old dago around. Shake hands with me, Waldo Hatch, and say you knew the last old wop. Then, when I'm done, there will be no more."

Gaetano felt ashamed of trying to trick the boy.

"Don't let anyone tell you about the old days, Waldo. Times were not better. We were too much with the church. Too much pain. We felt too much pain when people died. Wives would scratch at their faces. Throw their bodies on top of caskets."

"Gaetano?"

"Yes, son?"

"Will you have a flag on your casket as a war hero?"

Pain bolted through Gaetano's chest. At first he thought it was just the discomfort of hearing himself once again called a hero. But it lingered longer than the question.

"Mom! Mom!"

"Sshh, Waldo."

"Mom!"

"Sshh."

"Gaetano, Gaetano – what's wrong? Mom! Mom!"

"Sshh...come here, boy."

"I'm here. I'm here." The boy's voice shook and rose high and fast. "Mom, mom, Gaetano's sick!"

"Waldo," Gaetano panted. "Listen..."

"What?"

"Sshh...listen...."

"Okay," the boy whimpered.

"Listen..."

"Okay."

"Listen....no church, no flags. Waldo, I am not blind because I was brave. I am not blind because I was a coward. I am blind because we were all blind. Led by the nose."

His head fell back and he had difficulty breathing.

"Mom! Mom!"

Mrs. Hatch ran down the sidewalk calling to her son. Suddenly, Gaetano – in all his panting – belched so loudly that he and Waldo couldn't help but laugh and they were still laughing when Waldo's mother reached the porch.

Gaetano coughed and laughed but Waldo froze when his mother saw what was happening.

"Gaetano – oh my God!" she said.

"And they named a library reading room for me." Gaetano clutched his chest, coughed and chuckled some more. "Waldo, where are you?" he asked, even though he still held the boy's hand.

"Right here."

"And guess what, Waldo."

"What?"

"I never once read a book there!"

"Go get your father," Mrs. Hatch said. "Tell him to call 911 for Gaetano."

"Waldo, not one book!" He laughed. "Not one book! Laugh, Waldo! Give me a laugh!"

"Do as you're told!" his mother said.

"What? Laugh or get Daddy?"

"Go play football" said Gaetano.

"Tell Daddy to call 911 for Gaetano."

"What should I do? Gaetano, what should I do?" Waldo asked.

"Don't be led by the nose. If I go, I go. Don't be a hero. Go play football."

"Damn it, Waldo – go tell Daddy to call 911!"

Gaetano went limp. His hand shook softly on his stomach. Mrs. Hatch bolted into the house to call 911. She fumbled the phone, dropped it, cursed and then finally got through. The old man lifted his head.

"Waldo?"

"Yes?"

Gaetano let go of the boy's trembling hand. He smiled and leaned back and hummed. He lifted his hands like an orchestra conductor. Waldo watched for a moment, then felt free of worry. He stepped into the yard and lifted his face to the rain.

"Gaetano."

The old man did not turn to the boy but instead continued to conduct his orchestra. "I can hear it," Waldo said. "I can hear it now. I can hear St. Lucy's band."

Phone Call

The phone rang twice while Mary Stafford slept. She woke up on the third ring. The clock read 4:15 a.m. Her heart pounded. Her throat thickened. Who died?

Her mind shed its thick sleep in a panic. But her body forged ahead still in its uneven sleep, bouncing woozily off corridor walls. She thought of her old parents, her brothers and sisters. Who would be gathered at the house? Which sister would pick her up at the airport, a long hour's drive from her little town?

She filled her body with the power of a deep breath then picked up the phone.

"Yes?"

"Is Donny there?" said an urgent, distressed woman.

"Pardon me?"

"Is Donny there? This is Carla. I'm so sorry it's so late, but I have to speak to Donny." She spoke quickly, out of breath.

"There's no Donny here. You've dialed the wrong number," said Mary Stafford.

"Okay...all right," Carla said. Her voice cracked and after a moment, she hung up. Mary returned to bed, unable to sleep, but at least relieved no one she knew had died. Still, her heart rapped against her chest, her fear still smoking hot from its test run. She stared at the black phone in the hallway, illuminated by the full moon. What a miraculous invention, plastic and wires, that stops and starts hearts better than medicine.

"Poor woman," Mary whispered. Did Carla have bad news for Donny? Had one of Donny's parents died? Had Donny once loved Carla? Did he forget her? Did she hurt him? Was she calling so late because forgiveness could not wait? Was Donny, right this very second across town weeping, catching his breath? Was he laughing, bouncing on his bed, crying with joy – "Yes! Yes!" – and pulling another pillow from the closet?

Mary wrapped herself in a blanket, stood at the window and watched the crisp blot of yellow moon. Passing clouds gave it a misty, cheeky face that winked at the city. Mary imagined that during this moment each night, the throbbing city took its only respite. Its bleary-eyed night owls had just nodded off in armchairs, books on bellies, their sleep awash in the glow of snowy televisions. Early risers still twitched, drooled and mumbled in those soon-to-be-forgotten third acts of dreams. The gray jutting city bristled only sparsely with the star light, star bright twinkle of cabs, their fares dull-lidded sax players. And somewhere out there, Donny cradled the phone.

Mary returned to bed. She dreamed of moons, telephones, and Donny and Carla in a witching hour nuzzle. She dreamed of phone calls, the death of her parents, dreamed of tears shed alone, her apartment neighbors hearing her muffled grief next door, impotent to console her.

She dreamed of empty streets, dotted with firefly cabs and store window reflections of a million winking moons.

Then – blam – the phone. Mary opened her eyes and gone was the moon. The phone rang again. And again. Traffic honked. Sunlight stabbed her face. She found the clock.

"Ten thirty!"

The fourth ring.

It had to be work. She would be late again to a job she didn't like in a town that wasn't her home.

Her heart pounded. Her throat thickened. She breathed deep an empowering gulp and reached for the phone, trembling.

Vincent Semblia's Thanksgiving

Thirty-one Semblias lived in Zoalmont and it was traditional that every Thanksgiving Carmella Semblia hosted a big dinner for all her cousins, brothers, sisters–the entire family. Everyone brought something: a covered dish, some bread, a casserole, a bottle of homemade wine. It was truly a family event, a time when everyone pitched in to enjoy food and laughter.

Carmella's husband Carlo had died the previous spring but she amazed the family by insisting above all protests that she host the Thanksgiving dinner again this year. "We've got the biggest house," she said, settling the argument.

"Anything you want me to do?" asked her youngest, eleven-year-old Vincent, that Thanksgiving morning as he skipped out the door.

"Yes, as a matter of fact, yes!" she cried. "Vincent, come back here, I do have a chore for you."

Vincent was shaken. A chore? He was halfway across the lawn before his legs stopped. He was so accustomed to asking her just out of habit, to her saying no, shooing him off to play. But today, she wanted him to . . . do something?

"Vincent, come here," she said, pulling a five-dollar bill from her apron pocket. "Go to Wosnik's Market and bring me back some Parmesan cheese. Whatever you can get for five dollars, okay? Remember, they close at noon today."

Vincent was not used to this. His eight older brothers and sisters had always done the chores and fetched the last minute groceries. But now they were older, busy with their own lives, some married and living on their own, some overseas in the service, a couple of teen-aged sisters helping out in the kitchen, Vincent finally discovered what it was like to help pitch in.

His mother put her firm hands on his shoulders.

"Don't make that face. Don't make a major production out of it. Just go and do it. I know you wanna go be with your friends, especially that bad-news Homheinz. But this is a family day, Vincent."

The boy shrugged.

"You're not a little boy no more. Things ain't like last year. Your brothers are off on their own. Your sisters . . . well, they're your sisters. But you, Vincent, you're now the man of the house. Go get the cheese."

With the five dollar bill in his pocket, the boy ran a few blocks to the small downtown and met his friends behind Lotsky's Hardware store at the old swollen and cracked wooden doors of the empty warehouse. Vincent's two buddies were looking inside through holes.

"What's going on?" Vincent asked.

"It's damn near empty," said Sid Homheinz. "Lotsky's sold everything, man. There ain't a goddam thing left in there."

"That big store out by the highway killed this place," said Philip Berzansky.

"Yup, this place is empty," said Sid Homheinz. "It's about as empty as Berzansky's head!"

Sid laughed and poked his finger at Phillip Berzansky's skull.

"That hurts!"

"Then, go ahead, hit me!" Sid stood squarely in front of Phillip. "Hit me with your best shot."

"No," said Phillip.

"Why not?"

"Because I'm not stupid," said Phillip.

"I'm not so sure about that," Sid said, making a dufus face by protruding his already buck teeth out into Phillip's face. Then he noticed Vincent approaching. "Hey, it's my little buddy!"

Sid Homheinz was a confused brute. Philip Berzansky was a quiet boy who liked to read. Vincent was a little like both of them, but not enough of either.

Sid squeezed Vincent in a bear hug and swung him around.

"I'm getting dizzy, Sid."

"You my buddy?"

"I'm getting dizzy!"

"You my best buddy?"

"Yes!"

"You like me better than Berzansky?"

"I'm getting sick!"

"Answer!"

"Yes!"

"Okay." Sid let Vincent fly to the ground where he rolled once, then sat up and got his balance.

Philip extended a hand to Vincent.

"He ain't a girl," said Sid. "Don't treat him like a little pussy."

Vincent pushed the hand away. Sid walked ahead them toward the warehouse.

"Thanks anyway," Vincent said quietly to Philip.

Sid kicked at the door, which was padlocked. "Let's bust in. Let's loot the place. Maybe they got some old hammers laying around. We always need hammers at my house. My old man always takes a hammer every time he splits."

"I should probably get to Wosnik's," said Vincent. "I gotta get some cheese for my mom."

Sid lit up. "You got money? How much?"

"I really gotta go buy Parmesan cheese."

"Wosnik's is closed," Sid said.

"It's open till noon," Philip said.

"Shut up," Sid said, pushing Philip's shoulder.

"My mom said it's open till noon," Vincent said softly. He always spoke softly around Sid Homheinz.

His mother said that the Homheinz kid had a devil's hold on him. He was bad news. Lately she had been saying unusual things to Vincent. "Remember your father. However you behave in this town will be a reflection on your father's good name. Sid Homheinz doesn't care about good names. His father comes and goes from this town like the seasons. That's not you, Vincent. Remember you have a name. Vincent Semblia. Your father may be dead, but he never came and went like the wind."

"I gotta go to Wosnik's," Vincent said again.

"Jackerman's Bakery," said Sid in matter-of-fact disagreement.

"I gotta go to the store for my mom." Vincent's voice softened to an apology.

Sid Homheinz was disgusted. "You know those old Wosnik buzzards won't let me in their store. Thanks a lot, pal. Go to the places that won't let me in. Some true friend you are."

It was true. Once Vincent and Sid had walked into the store together. Mrs. Wosnick, a rotund, hard working woman who always wore a floral print dress the size of a small garden, smiled when she saw Mrs. Semblia's little boy. But when she saw who traipsed in behind him, her face froze in terror.

"I will not serve anyone until that kid leaves my store!" She pointed a wobbly finger to Sid, who mugged a face of disbelief. "We don't serve crooks here."

Sid yelled back, "You're nuts! You're a big, fat batty loon!"

"No, you're a thief," said Mrs. Wosnick. "You've stolen from this store so many times your grandchildren could owe me money!" She turned to the stockroom door in the back and called her husband. "Tom! The Homheinz kid is here and he won't leave!"

Mr. Wosnick waddled into the room. "Where's that little bastard thief?" His belly hung over his pants, barely held in place by his old stretched out t-shirt stained with the blood of fresh sausage meat. Mr. Wosnick shooed the boys outside, where Sid fired back a volley of profanities.

"Keep up with the guttermouth," said Mr. Wosnick. "I'll call the cops. Semblia, what would your father think?!"

"But I gotta go to Wosnick's," Vincent said.

"And I say, let's go to the bakery," Sid said.

Philip Berzansky tried to make peace. " Let's hike along the river. I read in a book about Zoalmont that up the river where it meets the railroad tracks there was a path that leads to the old hobo village."

"Homo village!" laughed Sid Homheinz. "That's perfect for you, Berzansky."

"Hobo village. Back during the Depression, which was in the thirties--"

"I know when the Depression was," Vincent interjected.

"Yeah, you know that but not everybody does," Philip said. "Anyway, in the Depression, there was lots of homeless guys without jobs who hopped trains. There was so many of them that they made little camps just outside of the towns where railroads went through. They could jump off the trains and be with other hobos. They'd all eat from a big black kettle of soup that was filled with wild onions and roots and potatoes they could find in the fields and they'd talk about towns they've been and who was hiring and–"

Sid Homheinz squawked. "You believe this bullshit?"

Vincent believed everything Philip Berzansky said because he knew Phillip read a lot.

"Berzansky's a fag and he's going out to the fag village by the railroad tracks. Is that where all the perverts go sleep at night, Berzansky?"

The bookish boy sighed and turned away. "You coming to the hobo village, Vincent?"

"I gotta go to the store," Vincent said with a smile to both of his friends.

Philip nodded. "After you go to the store. It's a short walk, out to Brackman's corner, can't be more than a mile."

Sid laughed, a little worriedly. "You believe his bullshit, Vinnie?"

"Come on, Vincent, I showed you all of this in the library book."

Vincent Semblia often walked past the hillside library where he would peek in the window and see Phillip hunched over books. If Phillip saw Vincent, he'd wave him in. But too often he was too engrossed in the book to notice.

"I don't know where he gets that stuff," Vincent said to Sid Homheinz. He looked away from Phillip.

"Come on, it's a really cool place," Phillip said.

"Donuts at Jackerman's!" cheered Sid. "Donuts! Donuts! Donuts!"

They walked quietly, the force of Sid leading them toward the bakery. Sid's confidence soared and he let fly some spit, hitting the toe of Phillip's sneaker. "Woops, sorry man. I was aiming for the dirt. Maybe I need glasses."

Flush with victory, he snatched Phillip's glasses and put them on, reeling and wobbling as he faked blindness.

"Don't break my glasses! Come on, man, my Dad'll kill me."

"Come on, man," Sid mocked. "Come on, man! "Your dad couldn't kill a kitten. Not like mine. Wah! Wah! Here's your stupid glasses. Let's get some donuts, man. I ain't had breakfast yet."

"It ain't my money," Vincent said quietly. Nobody listened.

"I'm going to the hobo village," said Phillip. He walked away, paused, and when no one joined him, kept walking.

The bells from St. Lucy's church chimed. Vincent panicked.

"It's noon! Wosnick's is closed!"

"We now have only one option," laughed Sid, wringing his hands like a villain in a silent movie.

They sat on the stoop in front of Jackerman's Bakery eating five dollars worth of eclairs and donuts and cream horns. A few minutes before Thanksgiving dinner began, Vincent straggled home, sick with fear and guilt and excess pastry.

Everybody was there, brothers, sisters, nieces, nephews, aunts, uncles, cousins, and one remaining grandmother. The air was filled with that holiday cacophony of laughter and unfinished sentences.

When it came time to eat, everyone sat at two long tables, one in the dining room and the other added in the living room for the day's feast.

Vincent sat as far away from his mother as possible and stared down at his plate. His father's oldest brother, Uncle Dominic, said bless-us-oh-Lord-and-these-thy-gifts. Everyone filled their plates, even Vincent. But he barely touched his food.

"What's the matter, Vincent?" his mother asked in his ear as she brought a gravy boat to his section of the kids' table. She looked at him with both concern and suspicion.

He mumbled something, looked away. She leaned in closer. "Vincent?"

He blurted out the words that had been sitting like heavy lumps in both his stomach and his mind. "I ate a bunch of donuts at Jackerman's."

He slapped his hand over his mouth. The table fell silent. Forks stopped in midair. The only sound was the dog's tail thumping the floor in excitement over the scent of gravy.

She leaned close to his ear. "And with who?"

She knew full well who.

Vincent poked at his plate. Talk, laughter and the clinking of plates resumed around the table but nobody commented on Vincent.

"Who did you say?" his mother said in even more of a whisper.

"Sid Homheinz."

She crossed herself and left the room. Vincent rose and followed her to the living room.

"What do you want?" she asked.

"I don't know. To say I'm sorry, I guess."

"Don't say it unless you mean it. If you mean it, I accept it. If you don't, you owe me five dollars."

"I mean it," he said.

"Good. Then you don't owe me the money. You're very lucky that your sister brought cheese and you should thank her."

"Maria?"

"Pierina," his mother said. "Maria brought the dinner rolls. You're very lucky that the rest of this family pitches in and helps me. But your luck is stretching thin, like a rubber band. Pretty soon it's going to snap. Then you'll be out of luck."

"I sure hate missing out on your delicious dinner," he said.

"Stop trying to butter me up. Don't even bother. You killed your appetite with those stupid donuts. Now you're trying to sweet talk me. 'I'm missing a good meal.' Is that all you're missing, Vincent?"

He didn't understand.

"That really makes me mad," said Vincent. "I'm missing this great dinner because of Sid Homheinz. I hate him."

"It's because of you," said his mother, poking her finger into his scrawny chest. "Sid Homheinz...he's just a boy like you. You're missing out on more than dinner if you blame the Sid Homheinzes of the world on everything."

Vincent ran outside and climbed the big oak tree in the yard. He shivered in the November cold and looked down upon his family through the dining room window. They praised the food and each other. Then he heard someone kicking an aluminum can up the street. He peered through the remaining dry, crumbling leaves to see Sid Homheinz ambling up the road, following the zig-zagging can, jamming on his air guitar. Sid did not see Vincent high in the tree. He knocked on the door. Mrs. Semblia answered the door. Vincent was surprised by his mother's courtesy.

"He's not in, sweetheart. He went out for a walk. He wasn't feeling well, so he went to get some air. Would you like something to eat?"

Sid responded quietly, then stared down at his feet. She said something again, then smiled quietly and closed the door, leaving Sid standing there scratching his head, looking around, wondering what to do next. Vincent could barely keep from laughing at his tough little friend, who looked so small and bewildered. And the thought that occurred to him next was so funny that he had to draw upon his emergency reserve of gravity, which he used mostly in school and church, to keep from giving away his hiding place by laughing. He gripped the branches, leaned back and unzipped his jeans. Below, Sid Homheinz felt the first drips, as if they were rain or dew from branches, and just as he looked up, the yellow stream sprinkled onto his head.

Sid recoiled, looked up and, in a second, started laughing. Vincent Semblia laughed, shook twice and climbed down, laughing so hard that he thought he would throw up the donuts.

"You should've seen your face!" Vincent said.

Sid lunged for Vincent and pushed him into the dirt. He wiped his face on Vincent's shirt and twisted Vincent's arm till it felt like it would pop.

"I ought to kill you," Sid said quietly into the same ear his mother had whispered into minutes before. Vincent groaned in pain but did not scream. He did not want his relatives rushing to the window. He prayed no one would see this. He imagined his father looking out the window into the yard seeing his youngest son getting shoved in the cold mud.

"What are you thankful for today?" Sid said, driving his knee into Vincent's back. Vincent began to cry. "Are you thankful for your friends? Huh? Answer!"

"Yes," sobbed Vincent.

"Say it! Say you're thankful for your best friend, Sid Homheinz!"

"I am..."

"Say it!"

"...thankful...for my...friend…"

"Best friend!"

"Best friend...Sid Homheinz."

Sid released him, stood up, took a few steps back. Vincent cried and gulped air. He didn't look up or move.

"You should be more thankful for your friends." Sid kicked Vincent's leg and spat on his back then walked through the back yard, down the narrow alleyway, and headed toward his own block and his own house with paint chips and bottle caps on the front porch and a cold stove in the kitchen.

Vincent climbed the tree again and watched his family eat and drink. His mother appeared at the door, her hands under a dish towel, her gaze worried and distant. It began to rain softly. Vincent climbed down and noticed he was too wet and filthy to go inside among all the guests. So he walked.

His only destination was anywhere but the street where Sid Homheinz lived. He reached the edge of town and heard a train whistle from out near Brackman's Corner. He thought he might hike out there to find the hobo village. Instead he roamed the wet black streets of Zoalmont till he could not longer put off sleep. Then he returned home.

Half the family was still there, warmed by wine, and stomachs stretched with too much good food, smiling in each other's glowing company, hands waving with old stories. Vincent snuck past them all like a wet dog, washed, slipped into dry pajamas, tip-toed into his mother's room and curled up to sleep on his father's side of the bed.

Far, Far From Home

We spat from the rooftop of the apartment building like honeymooners tossing pennies into Niagara Falls. Oh, what we discussed: Our love of sausage and Sammy Cahn, about old-fashioned love being taken over by people like us, who were not very old-fashioned in our swift and sweaty approach to it.

Though we tore at each other – *how does this unsnap...ouch, no – that's okay...a little this way* – our fangs were soft as cotton. Our smiles filled the dark corners with a rotogravure glow.

It began with chit chat and a so-so joint. But lest I give too much credit to marijuana, which after all, only intensifies what's there, let me sing the praises of your hands. When the words foundered, and our voices no longer led the discussion, it was your hand that took me away.

Your hand, cupping mine, at four a.m.

When night owls doze. When witches take their coffee breaks. When bread bakers take smoke breaks. When we exhausted our talk. When we knew each other's names but just that. When you took my hand and gave me a Peter Pan ride over St. Mark's Place. Like honeymooners we flew and pointed and never let go of each other's hand.

It was then I discovered that aphrodisiac is not

a word to waste on the label of a purple drugstore potion.

You can almost see the Statue of Liberty from here, you said as we huddled under the blanket in the foggy dawn.

I couldn't possibly have seen it through the mist. But I swear to you I did. I saw her arm jutting out like a lighthouse beacon, and I became an immigrant, new to myself, new to my senses; a pathetic but promising immigrant who tumbled weak and wet upon your shores, who would have to be taught everything new.

Waiting for the 23 Bus

A red light shone atop the intersection of Jasmine Court and Mulberry Avenue that hadn't been there five years before. While waiting for the light to turn green, the man riding on the passenger side of a landscaping truck lit a Salem and glanced out his window. He spat a sticky throatful onto the curb and squinty-glared at the lank, pale, orange-haired young man in a faded white tuxedo waiting at the corner. The rough-bearded landscaper flicked ashes in a McDonald's coffee cup and growled with contempt at the silly dandy on the roadside. The light turned green and traffic moved on, like a flooded river racing into a maddening ocean. Leo Snead stood still, waiting for the 23 bus.

A week before, Leo Snead's rusty fifteen-year-old Dodge Dart broke down on a highway exit close to where he worked at a video store. When that happened, he sat in the car for an hour, reading a magazine. He never considered getting out to hitchhike. He did not belong to an automobile club, so he could not get towed cheaply. He finally decided to gather all his belongings, unscrew the license plates and leave the car to be stripped by the spare-parts piranhas. He liked the old car, had a lot of fun in it, and felt the car could now be of use to others, a sort of automotive organ donation.

Also he knew nothing about cars, how to fix them or strip them, and he didn't want to bother with it anymore. There was nobility, he was convinced, in leaving valuable things lying around for others less fortunate to take. When he died, he would donate any needed organs to help others live. He was thinking of that as he stood at the corner waiting for the 23 bus. And Leo Snead was the type of young man who would abruptly speak as long as there was someone within earshot.

"I'm never buying another car," he said. "Does that mean I don't need to renew my driver's license? If that's the case, how will I make it known that I want to donate my organs after I die if I don't designate that fact on the back of my driver's license?"

The only other person waiting for the bus was an old, stooped Polish woman named Helen Borsky. She wore a black lace scarf over her head and an ornate brown wool sweater that had faded over the years but still looked elegant over her stout, hen-like body.

Helen Borsky was a woman who minded her own business. But when spoken to, she was not afraid to think deeply about what was being said, and in return, honestly speak her own mind. She was positive she had seen this gangly boy in the grocery store in her neighborhood. Helen Borsky figured if they bought food at the same place –

and now, they both waited together for the 23 bus – in addition to the plain fact that this young man had openly spoken to her first, then it would be fine to respond. She always made sure. In her youth she had been told many times by her neighbors to go home and mind her own business. Seventy years of practice and she still felt edgy, as if she would forget this rule. Which she often did.

"It's bad luck to talk about death being so young like you," she said, clutching her purse just in case. "And who knows, maybe you get a good deal on another car, huh?"

"So you think I should get my license renewed?" Leo Snead asked in earnest.

"Young people don't think!" Helen Borsky said. "Just because you got a driver's license don't mean you gotta drive. This isn't Nazi Germany."

Leo Snead played with his hair. "No. This isn't Germany. That's for sure." He extended his hand. "Hi, I'm Leo Snead."

"I'm Mrs. Borsky. Please to meet you."

Leo Snead leaned against the telephone pole and watched the two lanes of oncoming traffic. He wondered what would happen if he leaned out into this traffic just inches away. Would the line of traffic go with the flow and simply swerve around him, this human obstacle, this fleshy obtrusion? Or would the first car smack into him and the rest follow by flattening him into the asphalt like a groundhog. Just inches away. Only inches...

"Hey, how come you leaning so close!" Helen Borsky shouted.

Leo Snead pulled back and blinked. "Thanks. Whew, boy, what was I daydreaming! How long was I standing there? I'll bet I was in a magnificent trance." Leo Snead worried that his eccentricity might frighten the old woman.

Helen Borsky scoffed and shook her head at the absent-minded young man. "Don't be a fool. You was standing there five seconds, but I look in your eyes and you was in a different world." She wondered if he was on drugs. She could see that Leo Snead was not bothered in the least bit by her comments, so she continued to speak her mind. "What are you doing here at this bus stop? Why are you dressed up in that old tuxedo?"

"What am I doing? Why, what do you think? I'm catching the 23 bus!" He chuckled then burst into a short fit of shrill, barking laughter. Helen Borsky didn't laugh. Neither did she frown. She again shook her head and wondered about young people. What once was the simple, strange eccentricities of youth could now be the side effects of dope. Giddy kids weren't so cute anymore.

"Actually, I'm going downtown to find a job. Since my car broke down, I had to quit the job I had at the video store. Now I have to find a job near a bus line."

He wanted a job in an interesting office where creative people would appreciate his offbeat sense of humor. They would value his individuality – like this tuxedo – and say, "How ironic! You got the job, dude!" He'd be funny and befriend the secretaries.

Helen Borsky suddenly felt disgusted. "It makes me sick how bad the buses are in this day and age. All my life, I never learned how to drive a car. Never needed to. I could buy food down the street. The church was around the block. When we had to cross town, my husband, he could drive. Now he's gone. Now the store's a colored church. The people are nice, but no priest."

She poked her stubby spotted finger into Leo Snead's ribs.

"Mister, a bus every two hours is not good enough. There, I speak my mind. Now I mind my own business."

Leo Snead agreed that a bus every two hours was not good enough. He paused to take in Mrs. Borsky's face. It was small, hidden under the tightly-knotted scarf with a large nose, lips and pointy chin built on top like a banana split. Such character, thought Leo Snead. Except for her eyes. Her eyes were too small, too blue. Too steely blue. He wanted them to be brown.

Those eyes penetrated an abyss in front of

Helen Borsky, took her to a place only she could see, the plains of distant memories. She stood there for a long moment, shivering, nibbling her lower lip, her fuzzy jaw bobbing slightly, murmuring something in another language, perhaps a prayer. She wrung together her dark veiny hands. Leo Snead watched her closely, up and down, but did not stare at her shoes, for then he risked getting caught. Mrs. Borsky would surely reprimand him for being so nosy. Instead, he looked away and thought about how she looked. Her husband was dead and she had no one to drive her anywhere. The suburban buses stopped less frequently than the ones in town. And this stinking, honking, squealing traffic – spitting gravel and fumes everywhere – could give anyone a headache.

Poor Mrs. Borsky, thought Leo Snead. When sad, his face showed it. The old woman caught him gazing down at her vacantly with his silly pout.

"A young man like you. No job. No car. And now, you make a big baby face. Agh!" She waved him away disgustedly. "You should know pain. I don't wish it on you, but you should know it."

Leo Snead accepted this as a challenge to cheer her up.

"Watch this, Mrs. Borsky." He stood at the street corner and assumed a rigid pose. The busy, rusted-steel world circulated around him while he froze in time. He broke into the pantomimed character of an old, rubber-legged drunk. The old wino waved hello to imaginary passersby, tipping his top hat. Helen Borsky finally caught on to what Leo Snead was doing. At first she did not like it because it was unusual to see somebody performing like this at the bus stop, especially there on the corner of Jasmine Court and Mulberry Avenue, where everyone could see him. At first she was embarrassed and repeatedly looked away to the passing cars.

She tried to see the reaction of people in cars to Leo Snead's little comedy. But eventually, when Leo Snead came to the part where the old drunk finds an abandoned baby and tearfully cradles the child, Helen Borsky was held rapt. She floated back inside her own world, forgetting the loud traffic, oblivious to the distant, hazy city skyline. She was blind even to Leo Snead's sad clown face, dripping invisible tears over an imaginary foundling. Helen Borsky remembered other days, ones in which her husband clomped home heavy-heeled after an exhausting day at the steel mill. Days when that old doctor scolded her without mercy for trying and trying again to have babies when none would live. She knew that today's doctors could do something about it. But she would not want to be young today, not in this world, not for a million dollars. Young people had no respect for old people, or for that matter, no respect for each other. And there stood this Leo Snead, for no reason at all, bringing so beautifully to life a sad and secret part of Helen Borsky's past. The old woman shuddered, thinking this skinny boy with this outrageous hair wearing this Goodwill tuxedo, making such a spectacle of himself, was some spirit sent to mock her. Well, she would not be mocked. She harbored no regrets for her life and she told Leo Snead so directly.

"No more! No more! You're a bad actor!"

Leo Snead calmly broke character. "I'm not an actor at all. Oh, I must admit, there were times in high school when I entertained the idea. But I'm not much of a risk taker and an actor's life is full of risks. I wish I were more of a risk taker. Alas."

Leo Snead was pleased that he knew so much about himself.

Helen Borsky felt so much better hearing him say this. She knew that he was no spirit sent to taunt her. Once in a while, she needed reassurance that she was not insane. People thought that old folks were either dimwitted or wise, never anything in between. They seldom thought that old people could be afraid. Afraid of death maybe, they always allowed for that. Afraid of young punks, sure. But they never allowed old people to be afraid of their own demons. Young people hogged all these inner fears, these badges of self-pity. Old people were allowed to be only senile or only wise and to fear only one thing, death. Old people were not permitted to crave love. Old people in love disgusted young people. They wouldn't have it. They hoarded all the love in the world and let the old lovers starve.

She clutched her seventy-five cents bus fare and remembered scrimping to buy meat on holidays. Now, wherever she looked, there was a McDonald's, a Wendy's and a Ponderosa. Meat, meat everywhere!

"How come you don't get work here in the neighborhood in one of these meat places?" she asked Leo Snead. She motioned to all of the shiny new fast food restaurants lining the recently widened strip on Mulberry Avenue. Some neighborhood. Six lanes, high curbs, garbage food. Except for the fish sandwiches, she liked the fish sandwiches. Smelly delivery trucks, McDonald's bags.

Leo Snead did not answer. He was thinking about acting. He grew up juggling for his aunts and uncles. He begged for tap lessons but his father said no. Leo Snead's mother constantly scolded him for "showing off." He grew so self-conscious and full of doubt that he gave up singing and dancing and watched television all day. He learned how to pore over his thoughts dozens of times before uttering a word. It pleased him to know that no one knew him better than himself and he was delighted to help others understand him better if they so desired.

"The problem with you kids is that you're all too serious about yourself. I see on the news where a boy has a fight with his girlfriend, then he takes a rope and hangs himself. The teenagers drink too much beer, then they get killed. Listen to baby-baby-baby music – if you want to call that music – then you get so angry at the world, at everything. Really, now, the world is not so awful a place, once you get it into your head it ain't no tea party. It's all how you look at it to start with. If you don't expect roast beef steaks every Thursday, then when Thursday comes, and all you got is cabbage and maybe a slice of ham, you're not disappointed. I could tell you some almighty sad stories from back home, even before the Germans. But no one wants to hear them stories no more. Even I'm tired of thinking of those stories." Helen Borsky stopped and looked down at the sidewalk.

"I'm not a teenager," Leo Snead said, jerking his head away from her in an unfriendly way.

"So what. What I said, it's still true. You got the face of a tired garbage man. No, I take that back. I know a garbage man named Schmidt and he's not sad like you. He's tired but not sad. How come you so sad? Back there, you was acting as good as Charlie Chaplin. You know who that was?"

"Of course."

"You think you know. Watching movies on the television, knowing that they was special movies from sixty years ago...Leo Snead, that was different from seeing Charlie when he first come out, when you don't know what was gonna come next on the screen. Except one thing. We all knew we was gonna love it. We all loved Charlie. In my village, we was so excited when Charlie came on the screen. We sat in the big church watching the curtains. That was our movies, in the church, and up there on the white curtains was Charlie, wigglin' his mustache, makin' us laugh. Like an angel that come down to sit on our shoulder."

"I don't believe in angels," said Leo Snead. He did not mean to sound harsh or insult her beliefs. "I don't believe in ghosts, either."

"You've never been tested. Have some pain, some sickness, then tell me there's no devil or angels."

Six little babies. All dead. A husband who worked too hard and loved too little. He did not hit her. He did not hug her. Ahh, maybe he did love her after all. Who could be sure? The only blessing she could think of was that in all her eighty-two years, she never needed glasses. With those strong eyes she peered into the sky. Hard winds pushed dark clouds toward town. She felt for her umbrella. It would be raining when she stepped off the bus.

She turned away from Leo Snead and looked toward the traffic. If she stared into it long enough she felt drawn in, sucked into an undertow. That frightened her. The 23 bus was late.

"Where are you going?" asked Leo Snead.

She did not hear him.

"Mrs. Borsky."

"What?"

"Are you going somewhere special?"

Helen Borsky looked at him. "I am going to babysit my great-grandson. He's a looker. Two years old he is, strong as an ox." She knew if that were true, the boy would be strong, like her husband.

"Good. I'll bet you're a wonderful great-grandmother." Leo spoke with a flourish, like a big egg-colored ostrich flapping about in excitement. He hoped his concern would please her.

"Yeah, yeah," she said without emotion.

It did not bother her one bit to lie. Leo Snead seemed happy that she was going to babysit her great-grandchild. He did not question her any further. Leo Snead was himself preoccupied, worried about being late for his appointment at the temporary agency downtown. He hoped to find a temp-to-hire position somewhere in the downtown area near a bus line so he would never again have to worry about auto maintenance, parking, insurance. He could buy a monthly bus pass and maybe if he rode the same time everyday, he would meet someone and they would fall in love. Anything was possible in an old-fashioned world. And riding the bus seemed as old-fashioned as you could get in an American culture that guzzled fossil fuel like sodas.

"We're ruining our environment with the fumes of the internal combustion engine," murmured Leo Snead.

"It's been ruined longer than you think," said Helen Borsky. "Society is going to hell. Kids who kill themselves got nothing over on us for bright ideas on how to escape it all. We never thought about killing ourself, but we sure felt like it. We had reasons. We was knocked over by death, death and more death, and sickness and hatred every day, back home. But we wasn't quitters."

Leo drew a breath to say that it was his generation who grew up with the looming specter of the Bomb, but come to think of it, he could think of no one who cared about war or even peace.

"Keep your Phil Donahue!" said Helen Borsky. "Keep your Sally Jesse. Keep your Okrah. I wouldn't take a ton of gold to be young again!"

Helen Borsky saw the 23 bus idling at the red light at the intersection near the K-Mart.

"There used to be in this world too many children and no meat and no cars. Now times change. What was white is black. Now there's too much meat, too many cars, and the children, well, they're no use to nobody. Do you gotta be poor and sick to care about who lives next door?

Times have changed for the worst, I tell you. What was white is black."

"The slow ones now will later be fast," Leo Snead sang. "The times, they are a–changing."

"Huh?"

Helen Borsky was glad that Leo Snead would get off the bus before she did, downtown, so that she could ride on to the west side, her old neighborhood from when they first came to America. Now it was rough and dangerous, filled with barred grocery stores, churches, crack houses, bars with front door signs stating NO GUNS PERMITTED.

She was headed for one of those churches. It used to be her church. The only thing to remind her was the stained glass. There she would say a prayer to Mother Mary, then walk down the street to the hospital where she cuddled and fed babies born sick and addicted. An 82-year-old and an 8-day-old keeping each other warm. Then she would walk outside and wait...clinging to her purse like the babies clung to life...wait for the 23 bus, to take her way back home to the little apartments behind the big shopping plazas outside of town, where a nurse visited Helen once a week and where there were sidewalks only in front of big stores.

She was relieved that Leo Snead got off before her, before even his own scheduled stop. He wouldn't make it to his appointment. How could the temp firm possibly understand his passion for creativity? He needed a job, yes, but today he could afford to let his individualism live for one more day outside of a cubicle.

Instead, Leo Snead roamed from store to store, browsing at used records and books while Helen Borsky sang Polish lullabies to screaming, exhausted babies withdrawing from addiction.

"What a waste," Helen Borsky thought, looking down at an infant's callow brown cheek. She thought of her village, the fires of war, the many years of meals shared with a man she didn't know...life with no babies of her own...buses that ran like they were doing her a favor...silly Leo what's-his-name.

"What a waste," she thought, but continued to sing softly, "Ach spij kochanie."

Sleep, my darling.

Stupid

Everything about the interview was stupid. She wore a stupid blue suit, was up for a stupid sales job. Sat there awkwardly, nodding like a lapdog, giving dumb answers to questions asked by a dopey round-faced man with no hair and a wet lip. On his desk, stupid placards:

You want it by when?

You don't have to be crazy to work here, but it helps.

So stupid she wanted to scream, but screaming would be stupid. She needed the job. She had two children to feed and an ex who renounced money and lived in a leaky tugboat trying to find himself. She couldn't even sell their house for a decent profit. Bad move, buying that house. How stupid of them to think the neighborhood was on the upswing.

How her stupid blue power suit itched. But her smile exuded confidence. She crossed her legs and was careful to listen and not speak too much, not finish the man's stupid sentence.

You'd have to pay a third of your major medical, he told her, but the commission rate is great.

Reasonable, she answered, eager but cool.

She smiled and arched a brow when Mr. Poopbreathbaldhead outlined the job duties. She nodded when other workers – the bored and boring momentarily free on probation from cubicles, passed by in the hall, checking her out.

"Now, Mrs. Brill, here is a question that will require some thought," he said. "We've gone over your strong points. What would you say is your weakest trait?"

She stammered, pinned under the thumb of Mr. Ladderclimbinglackey. Her eyes darted about nervously.

What a stupid question!

Oh, oh, oh whatever could it be? That she tries too hard? That she stays at the office late into the night to finish her work? My flaw, she could say, is that I come to work too early, invoking the wrath of fellow employees, but that's something I can live with, sir, because soon everyone shows up early and the company benefits! My flaw is that I'm here on Sundays, separating the entangled paper clips! Or, I make such damned good coffee that during my vacation the whole company rejects their own repugnant coffee and production plummets by 37% on *good* days!

"Weakest trait? Tough one..."

That I cannot help but massage the boss and do his laundry. I just can't help it! It's my weakness!

Mr. Bigbellyballpoint leaned back. What was he thinking? Too slow on her feet? Indecisive? Jowly?

She let that son of a bitch charge everything on her cards, and then he decides to go find himself. Worst of all, he looked better than ever.

Mr. Middlemanagementuglytie twiddled his pencil and snuck a glance at the clock. He was waiting. Time was money.

She looked at him close and hard. They shared that smirk, him across the desk and him on the leaky boat. What would it be like working here? She'd go home spitting, in tears, and with all these young chippies flouncing around, she'd be reminded that she was old, broke, out of fashion, and unable to remember her last ecstatic romp. Who needed this?

She closed her eyes. She envisioned herself a caterer, a stunning and svelte server of cake, taking the torch of kitchen expertise from the old Italian ladies, thanking all the old men at the banquet for their compliments, apologizing for not being permitted to go dance with them, laughing her laugh that could only be described as the cross between a hundred champagne glasses clinking in a toast with an orchestra consisting of three dozen babies being tickled.

"My weakest trait? Well, I sometimes steal out of the petty cash drawer to buy crack."

He blinked and drew back. But he listened. His face oozed slowly into a knowing smile. He nodded his head affirmatively, gave her a gentle wink and extended his hand to welcome her aboard.

Air Guitar

Teaching is jazz, thought Arlo McGill, when the soul takes over the mind, the fingers twiddle free, and the guitar's flourish is magic. There he stood, free from lecture notes, unafraid of forgetting his Teacher Manual answers, in front of and not behind the desk, hands flailing in the rapturous throes of his solo. Student daydreamers awoke to jam on their young teacher's eloquent wail.

Just months before, Arlo McGill himself had been in their seats, an undergraduate in search of orgasmic truth. When it eluded him, he did the logical thing. Enrolled in graduate school. For months he had floundered, muffing his lectures, talking big, not being himself. But now came the miracle breakthrough. Without thinking, he spun a fine web of wisdom and it hung in the air over the classroom like a divine mist.

He compared rap to sonnets, Tennyson to Jim Morrison, Oscar Wilde to Elvis Costello. His students cocked their heads, rapt. For the first time since he began teaching, Arlo McGill felt capable of flight.

Suddenly, Jerome Baldy's chair collapsed.

This rotund freshman always sat in the thick middle of the classroom. As if he somehow weighed more at the room's center, the chair beneath him imploded. The plastic and aluminum simply gave, without a wobbly warning, leaving Jerome Baldy sprawled on the dirty linoleum floor, tangled in the twisted legs and cracked desktop, aflame with embarrassment.

Jerome Baldy groaned and cursed the injustice of it all. He flung broken bits of desk out of the way and rocked himself to his feet. For a second all jaws dropped. Then as if they had no choice, the entire class howled with laughter. A few attempted composure, but the suppression of laughter led their shoulders to shake and their faces to redden even more than Jerome Baldy.

Jerome raised himself up, looked at every face in the room and said, "Yeah, I know, I gotta start passing on dessert."

This all happened so quickly that Arlo McGill had also erupted in laughter. He did not rush to Jerome Baldy's side. He did not help Jerome to his feet, nor lift those commanding hands in a gesture for all to shush. Instead, the teacher's horsey laugh intruded into that divine mist above the room. In just seconds, his lecture became smoke and mirrors. His maturity dissipated like the belief in magic once the magician packs up his trunk and is seen grunting and lifting it into the back of a station wagon.

Jerome Baldy found another desk and comically tested the chair's ability to hold his weight. His classmates supported him with warm, affirmative chuckles. A few of them asked if he was okay. Arlo McGill attempted to continue his lecture, but no one listened.

Tradition

Vinnie Russo looked down upon the village of Zoalmont. It was wedged between two hills like a helpless infant who would forever suckle but never grow. When he was a boy, smoke hung in the air. Factory whistles sliced through the air three times a day. Vinnie would miss a few lines of dialogue watching Howdy Doody when the closest whistle blew. Then came the tramp-tramp of his father's work boots and the cling-clang of his mother's pots and pans.

It began to rain. As kids, they watched the hilltop from the town below, hoping that lightning would touch down. They told stories about how the electric bolts that split the sky would crack open the doors of crypts, setting free their long dead grandparents and great-grandparents and ancient aunts and uncles to roam the cemetery.

Today it did not thrill or frighten Vinnie Russo. As the hard rain fell he leaned against the gravestone he had come to see.

Born 1917. Died...

He wondered how much it would cost to have that death year chiseled in.

Vinnie rested his heavy body down in the mud and raised the pint bottle to his lips. He leaned back to let the rain wash over his oily, hairy face. The topsoil of the freshly dug grave became soupy with mud, but Vinnie Russo did not move. It wasn't because he was drunk – though he was very drunk, as he often was drunk – but because he was comfortable and at peace, away from the town with crumbling foundries and cheap rent, with its seven church steeples and, from where he was sitting, the speck of a rippling flag above the post office. The town where he did nothing much more than drink and duck from ex-wives who were as poor and trapped as him and who got uglier and meaner each day. Like him. At that moment he wished to be swallowed up in the mud, joining his father in some promised land.

Then an engine sputtered. Vinnie opened his eyes. An olive green BMW approached. Vinnie rolled out of the mud and hid behind his father's grave. A man about Vinnie's age sat behind the wheel. Even though heavy clouds darkened the sky, the driver wore sunglasses and a brimmed hat. The car stereo – a loud, anxious ad for a Ford dealership – competed with the lull of raindrops and distant thunder.

The driver snapped off the radio and stepped out of the car. He pushed a button in the palm of his hand and a black umbrella crisply snapped open. Vinnie Russo didn't know name brands, but he could tell that the raincoat and umbrella and probably the hat were the finest he had ever seen.

Was it him?

"Vinnie?"

It was him. Well. He came after all.

Vinnie stood, approached the car, caked in mud. His peace had taken wing and headed south. Now all he felt was cold and stupid and drunk. He slipped the bottle into his back pocket.

"Vinnie?"

"Kirk." Vinnie extended his hand. Kirk saw the grimy hand, he put his umbrella in his right hand and pointed to his father's grave with his left hand.

"Is that it?"

"That's it," said Vinnie, withdrawing his hand, even hiding it behind his back.

"I can't believe it."

"Seeing's believing," Vinnie said. "It's been a week."

"I just found out," said Kirk.

"We called," said Vinnie. He had spoken to his younger brother about once a year and it always made him nervous. Kirk was either graduating from college or getting married or passing the bar or moving to another city or winning a case or buying a bigger house or...

Well, while all this was going on, Vinnie was either farting on barstools, or working under the table as some carpenter's gopher, or hunting for his necktie to wear to court to kiss up to some judge every time he was behind in child support.

"Still welding?" Kirk asked.

Welding? Welding?

Vinnie blinked, and then remembered that he had once lied to Kirk about being a welder.

"We called about Dad. Funeral was last week."

"I got the message on my machine," Kirk said. "I was in Europe for two, three weeks."

"Was it two? Or three?"

"Look, I just got back. As soon as I heard, I..."

He stopped talking and glared at Vinnie. It was a showdown. The dark glasses made Vinnie nervous so he pulled out his bottle.

"Well, I'm here now."

"Take off those sunglasses," Vinnie said, gesturing to the dark, cloudy, rain-filled skies.

Kirk surprised Vinnie by obliging him. He removed the glasses. Vinnie felt his brother's eyes pounce. Kirk said not a word but his eyes mocked Vinnie, told him how fat and smelly he was, how the crack in his ass showed when he bent over, how anyone within five feet could get a good whiff of him.

Kirk held out his hand for the bottle.

"You'll take this but not my hand?"

"Come on," Kirk said impatiently.

"Not your brand," Vinnie warned him, but then gave up the bottle. Their hands met around the glass neck, smooth pink bejeweled fingers next to bruised and cracked ones, ten fingers and two hands that once climbed baseball bats to choose up sides.

Kirk drank some then pulled a grocery bag from his car and took it to the grave. He pulled out a loaf of brown bread and a small brick of cheese. He broke each in half and gave some to Vinnie.

"Pop's favorite snack," said Kirk, holding the bread up in the rain. "It's traditional to eat the deceased's favorite food at the gravesite."

Kirk bit and chewed. It's also traditional to go to your father's funeral, thought Vinnie.

"Vinnie, grab the wine." Vinnie reached into the grocery bag and held up the bottle with no label. "Homemade? Whose?"

"Dad always made his own. Remember how he'd go load up the truck with Lake Erie grapes?"

"This is his wine?" Vinnie asked.

"No, but it's homemade. I bought it from a farmer I met in Sicily. His name was Gaitano Giovanni Battista Pizzarello. What a melodious name!"

Vinnie looked away.

"Dad would like this," Kirk said.

"Dad would've liked a visit from you when he was sick. Did you even know how sick he was?"

"I knew exactly what was going on."

"You could've showed your face. Instead you bring wine made by a guy with a whatever-odor name." Vinnie was nervous. If only he had something to shove into Kirk's face, or some accomplishment, some stunning wife, or even a marriage that lasted. Hell...a job. All he had was his bedside devotion to their father.

"You could've showed your face," he said again.

"I have a life," he said. Kirk smiled, took a corkscrew from his jacket pocket, and twisted it into the cork. "If you had one yourself, you'd understand." He popped the cork.

"I have a life, too." Vinnie drank from his own bottle. Kirk took a long gulp of wine, and then pointed the bottleneck toward the small town at the bottom of the hill.

"There? That's your life?" Kirk almost chuckled. Instead took a long, deep, sad breath. "Speaking of faces, I saw a fat kid, about twelve, standing in the front of the bank. Looked just like you."

"Yeah, well, probably is. Where the hell should he be? Where should he hang out?"

Kirk laughed. "My own nephew. And do you know what he did? He gave me the finger. Saw my car, flipped me the bird. If he would've known who I was..."

"He'd of done the same thing," Vinnie said. "He always talks about taking an Uzi to all the rich bastards out there."

"Nice kid."

"He lives with his mother."

"Della?"

"No."

"Not Della?"

"Marilyn," Vinnie said.

"Your...third?"

"Second. I only got married twice."

Kirk nodded. "I thought three."

"I lived with Sandy for a while," said Vinnie.

"Sandy...?"

"Pottsdamm. Sandy Pottsdamm."

"That's who I thought number three was," said Kirk, "from Mom's Christmas cards. So, how many rich guys does he even see cruising through town?"

Vinnie changed the subject. "You still married?" Vinnie asked. Kirk laughed.

"It's nice you should ask, Vin. But really, who cares? What are you doing up here in the rain? Why aren't you at the house?"

"I'm grieving." His voice sounded fake. He didn't know what to say. Kirk looked at his lumpen brother. "The only thing you'll grieve is when that bottle's empty." Kirk snatched it from Vinnie's hands and downed it in two gulps. "How can you drink this piss?"

"I don't have ritzy taste. Don't have any money. But I was here!"

"So you were here. And look. He's still dead."

"He suffered for a long time. At the end, he was nothing but a skeleton with red eyes. Coughing. All boney fingers. Crying all the time. You should've come to see him, Kirk."

Kirk looked away disgustedly. Suddenly he threw the bread and cheese into the mud on top of his dead father.

"Some tradition," said Vinnie.

"For what, Vinnie? I should have come for what? Could I have saved him?"

"You owed it to him," Vinnie said.

Kirk balled his fists and circled Vinnie. Vinnie lurched, frightened, even though he could easily maul his brother. At least he thought he could. Kirk was a softie. It was not Kirk's fists that frightened Vinnie, but his quick tongue. His words that jabbed like a boxer.

"I owed him what, Vinnie?"

"You owed him..."

Vinnie could not think. He prayed for words. "You owed him your life. You owe your parents your life because life is what they gave you."

Kirk gritted his teeth and wiped rain from his eyes. Mud smudged his cheek. "I owed him one thing, Vinnie. My ears. I listened to what he said when I was a kid. What he told me about hard work. And standing up for yourself and getting ahead. I owed him my ears. And I did listen. I listened to his stories about leaving Germany, walking eighty miles to the train, coming here with one cardboard suitcase. His journey set me on my own path. I kept his journey going. I've been to Germany, to his village. It's our village, too. I've met our relatives. Do you know what they told me? That his own father was sick in bed while Dad was here. This is how it works."

"He'd ask about you, I'd be at the hospital, trying to say stuff to him. All the machines and tubes would make me so nervous and scared, which made him even more scared, too. I wouldn't know what to say. That's when he'd ask about you. 'When's Kirk coming?' he'd say, coughing up everything. He knew you could talk to him about stuff and get his mind off dying."

Kirk turned toward the town below.

"Then why did you come?" Vinnie asked. "There's nothing much in the will."

"I just found out! I was traveling! I didn't check my machine! You wouldn't understand. You know, he always told us to get out of Zoalmont, make something of ourselves, see the world. No, you just wouldn't understand."

"Don't you wish you could've told him goodbye?"

"Are you really curious to know the answer to that? Is this a real conversation? Or are you trying to make me feel like shit?" Kirk's eyes burned into his brother. Vinnie could not think.

Kirk reinserted the cork into the wine bottle and stuck it in the mud next to the bread and cheese.

"We ought to bury this and come back every year and take a drink," Kirk said.

"Sounds too much like a tradition," Vinnie said.

Kirk softened. "I don't hate tradition, Vinnie. Tradition requires passion. Eating sauerkraut on New Year's Day is not tradition. Tradition is passing on strength. Okay, don't listen."

"I'm listening." Vinnie hated a lecture.

"Pop left Germany because he was hungry. He had dreams. All his friends were over there goose-stepping and he was here on his own terms. No, I didn't visit him when he was sick. But if he could see us now, who would be most proud of?"

"His boney fingers held on to me for hours. I held him in my lap like he was a baby. He wore a diaper. And now you say he'd be prouder of you because you're wearing that suit?"

Kirk blinked and swallowed. "I'm going back to the house. Coming?"

Vinnie looked away.

Kirk speared the umbrella into the ground. "Stay dry."

Without looking back, Kirk got in the car and sped off. Vinnie watched his brother race through the town's streets and pull into the Russo gravel driveway.

The rain stopped. The sun went down. Vinnie pulled the wine from the mud and finished it. He killed a little time by bending and snapping each spine of Kirk's umbrella, poking each one into the ground, making a fence around his father's grave. The cold wind howled. Quiet heat lightning lit the sky. In flashes, Vinnie could see the graves. He shook – in fear, in cold – and imagined the dead, even his father, hunkered behind their stones, creeping in around him in the dark. He was scared, but he stayed, till he heard in the Sunday silence the mosquito hum of his brother's car pulling out of their mother's driveway a quarter mile away.

Teeth chattering, toes numb, hangover begun, he watched the headlights race through Zoalmont's quiet Sunday streets, crawling through stop signs, anxious for the freeway.

Hard to Please

The phone rang a third time. Vernon Murtzer turned to his wife.

"Whose turn is it?"

"Mine," said Helen Murtzer. "But you answer it."

"I always do."

"So let it ring," she said.

"It's not my turn but I'll answer it. Why do we bother with the rule?" Vernon reached for his cane. Helen read a magazine, moving her lips.

"Suit yourself," Helen said. She lifted the magazine close to her eyes. "I need new glasses."

Vernon plonked over to the phone and picked it up.

"Damn it all," said Helen as she squinted into her magazine. "I'll probably get new glasses, then I'll die. Wouldn't that beat all . . . don't shush me, Vernon."

"I'm on the phone," Vernon said in a voice soft as butter.

"Just don't shush me."

"Okay, but I'm on the phone."

"Fine, just don't shush me like that."

"All right, already. Hello? Hello? Charley? Oh my Lord, it's Charley! Good to hear you, Charley. Helen, it's Charley!"

"Well hello to Charley, but I will not be shushed."

"You're coming to town?" Vernon said excitedly. "Helen, Charley's coming to town."

"When?" asked Helen.

Vernon turned his attention to the phone.

"When? Vernon, when?"

Vernon motioned for her to be quiet.

"When's he coming? When's Charley coming?"

"Charley, hold on a second." Vernon cupped the phone. "The twenty-eighth," he told his wife.

"No, absolutely not!"

"What? Oh, Helen, what in damn hell? Charley, hold on for a second, please."

"You have to ask why?" Helen said.

"You're kidding me."

"Nope."

"You...are...kidding me!"

"Bring me the Bible," she said, her hand raised.

"Change your appointment," Vernon said.

"Yolanda expects us on the twenty-eighth of each month," Helen said. "So does Traveler's Lodge. It's a habit. It's a standing appointment. I don't change good habits."

"I haven't seen my brother in..."

Vernon bit his tongue, clenched his jaw, and considered punching a hole through the drywall but he knew his wrist would snap like a saltine.

Instead, he uncupped the phone. "Charley? Sorry to keep you. No, no trouble at all. Just another second, okay?" Vernon covered the phone again with his hand. "It's a long-distance call, Helen." He glared at her but his chin shook. "This is my brother!"

"I know who Charley is," said Helen.

"My only brother. Who I haven't seen in nine years."

"Tell him to come on the twenty-seventh. Or the twenty-ninth."

"He's with a tour group. It's a sightseeing bus. They're making a three-hour stop at the wood carving museum. That's it!"

Helen shook her head no.

"Get your hair done another day. How many hairdressers do we have in this town? Why does it have to be Yolanda?"

"She knows how I like it," Helen said. "She's the only one so far who's got it right."

On the 28th of every month, they drove two hours to Philadelphia with a standing reservation at a Traveler's Lodge off one of the less commercial suburban exits. All so Yolanda Davis could do Helen Murtzer's hair.

Yolanda moved to Philadelphia so her husband could receive therapy for all his strokes, Helen said, "Why are you so heartless with the infirm?"

"Heartless? That's baloney. I knew Pete Davis before all his troubles, when he could run the bases faster than kids half his age. Remember when the King and His Court came to town, played that fast pitch game at the state fair? Who was the only to get a hit off the King? Pete Davis is who!"

"That's what makes it worse. You remember Pete in his prime. And yet, you think I should just trade in Yolanda for any old hairdresser in town."

Vernon shook his head, heaved a deep sigh, and put the phone back up to his face. "Charley? Sorry to keep you. Can I beg you for just one more little second?"

Vernon squeezed a pillow around the phone.

"Helen, this is why we missed his wife's funeral, too, for your dang hair! I just thank God Charley forgave me for that."

"Yes, thank God," Helen agreed.

"Charley? No, there's no problem. What?" Vernon mouthed he heard you.

Helen put her feet up on the stool. She wiggled her toes. Vernon stammered on the phone, but Helen could hear Charley's voice on the other end of the line, squealing like an agitated rodent. Then – click – the yelling stopped. Vernon replaced the phone. His bifocals slid down his nose.

"Is Charley mad?"

Vernon would not answer.

"Well, is he mad?"

Vernon looked away.

"Is he or is he not angry?" Helen asked calmly.

Vernon shot a quick look at Helen, a dart of disgust. As a boy he worked on railroads under bulls who brutally beat lazy workers and even killed at least one tagalong hobo. He hated every railroad foreman he ever met. As a young man he fought a bloody war in Europe and came nose to nose with more blood and death than anyone should ever see. His best buddies died horribly. He fired bullets into abandoned busts of Hitler. He hated the Germans and he hated Hitler. How often he had wished his heart dry for them to suffer in hell. But never had he felt such an intense death wish upon someone than when he snuck that quick look at Helen.

"You just hate me, don't you?" she said, a little too musically.

Vernon walked away.

"Vernon, if you're going into the bedroom, bring back my slippers. My tootsies is cold."

Vernon sat on their bed and stared at Helen's lumpy, banana-yellow slippers. Helen waited patiently on the couch, flipping through magazines, humming every show tune she knew, including TV show theme songs, which she counted as show tunes.

Forty-five minutes later, Vernon Murtzer delivered her slippers.

"I just hope you're satisfied," he said. "I hope your conscience is clear."

"Thanks for my slippers," she said, kissing the air five times for Vernon, who waved her away.

"Helen, you're too hard to please." He fixed a hard stare at her. She looked at him lovingly. The hallway clock struck eight, Vernon's cue to go to the kitchen, fill the kettle with water, turn on the stove, and get two tea bags ready.

Who's Going to Help Uncle Vincenzo Stir the Polenta?

I need a flexible work schedule to accommodate my college classes. That's why I love working at Angelina's. She lets me make my own schedule. I'm not even sure I'm a good prep cook or waiter. What matters to Angelina is my hands. All I ever had to do was use my magic fingers on her tight shoulders, kneading them like her prized dough. "Awwwgh!" she would squawk in pleasure. "Awwwgh! Genie, you got a good thing going there." Angelina's husband Rocco never massaged his wife's stiff shoulders. "You're married as long as I been," he told me once, "and you don't touch your wife no more than you got to."

That night, I asked Angelina if I could get off work early. She looked at me, turned around, and knowingly pointed a finger to her neck. Without a word, I rubbed and squeezed all the tension out of her while she crowed and moaned as if the sky were splitting open and God himself was her masseur. I wanted to get off work early in order to make it on time to my aunt and uncle's house for fresh helpings of polenta. I dared not tell Angelina why I wanted to leave early. Italian cooks are proud. She was not offended when her husband said that he did not want to touch her body. But had Rocco said to her that he was sick of her food, and then she would have murdered and divorced him – in that order. I could not tell my lovely stout boss Angelina that I was forsaking her that night for my Uncle Vincenzo's annual polenta fest. After all, hadn't Angelina entrusted me with her sauce recipe? I say no more. Baking pizza is an art. There are enough awful fly-by-night pizza joints out there for you to know this. They think that by putting a magnetic WE DELIVER sign on the car, anyone can make a profit. Well, perhaps they can. To paraphrase P.T. Barnum, no one ever went broke underestimating the American WASPs appreciation for Italian cuisine. The Sicilian square, crunchy and thick – the Chicago deep-dish, fat as a one-layer cake only this cake holds no candles – the thin and crispy New York style that you fold up and eat while you hurry down the sidewalk – these are baked works of art. But here in modern America big business and the arts mix and that is an incongruity. For instance, the best scenes in movies are the ones we never see, the ones I'll bet which are edited out by the cowards who finance the projects. And I find something obscene in a Picasso selling for $25 million or a Van Gogh for nearly $60 million. I know, I know, art has always been an investor's medium, but this kind of money used to represent things like, say, our national debt – not an Impressionist painting. And look at the growth of chain pizza places – Domino's, Pizza Hut, Little Caesars. Go ahead, tell me that you are eating authentic Italian food. Face it, since the last wave of European immigration ended in the middle part of this century, we are all a bunch of homogenized suburbanites, our taste buds unable to detect, let alone appreciate ethnic authenticity. The only cultural acknowledgement I can imagine any of us mainstream Americans remotely experiencing when it comes to food is a startled reaction to getting a round-eyed waiter in a Chinese restaurant. We don't expect the Taco Bell kid to speak Spanish, do we?   Let me put it this way: I work at Angelina's Ristorante. But also, I work for Angelina herself. She signs my checks. When I finish afternoon classes, zip across town in my trusty, rusty Valiant, I walk into the back door, under the sign which reads ANGELINA'S. I wash up and then work side by side with that very Angelina. There is Angelina, slicing pepperoni. Answering phones. Hauling flour sacks from the stockroom. Boxing carryouts. Scolding the delivery men for being late.

Angelina mopped the floors, cleaned the stoves, and she was one of the few people I knew not afraid to tell teenagers not to talk so loud.

Because she still speaks with a trace of Italian accent and her entire approach to work and life is Old World with an almost religious fervor, it may surprise you when I say that Angelina is America. She is rugged individualism, not that stupid different-for-different's-sake individualism, tantamount to simply wearing T-shirts emblazoned with SHIT HAPPENS or driving around with bumper stickers reading IF YOU DON'T LIKE MY DRIVING, CALL 1-800-EAT-SHIT. No, Angelina is America because there is no one else like her and there is only one Angelina's Ristorante. America is like the world's junk drawer, where anything and everything is thrown in. America was not meant to be a series of identical landmarks duplicated along interstate highway exits every ten miles. What has McDonald's given us besides that Mc-prefix which means tacky and inferior? The blanding of America has made inferiority the new mediocrity. The advertising copywriter is now the chic arbiter of art rather than what he used to be, the huckster of popular taste. The ad hack is now hepdom's gauge, where once hepdom was something to be earned by being subtle and perceptive and witty, (not to mention well-read,) not by being able to name all of the Brady kids. I've been doing some reading and I am convinced that a large TV monitor over the bar would have silenced the Algonquin Round Table.

I enjoy my classes at college, and I enjoy my work baking pizza and cooking tomato sauce, for it allows me to dwell in my thoughts, which are such as these, and which drive me to distraction and oftentimes lead me to consider life as an expatriate. But Angelina – her presence, her fantastic sauce! – keeps me here. Only one thing tops the innovative beauty and originality of America, and that is – now, *was* – the annual polenta dinner at the home of my father's aunt and uncle, Roberta and Vincenzo Castelluci.

I made up an excuse, mumbled something about a history exam, and finished rubbing Angelina's neck and shoulders. When I arrived at my aunt and uncle's house, the air held the smell of sauce like a morning cloud sponges in the moisture of the afternoon cloudburst. I said hello to my parents, who were on their way out for a stroll to the corner store for some frozen yogurt.

"Who's here?" I asked.

"Just us," my father said. "Your sister and the twins, too. Uncle Vincenzo's kids couldn't make it this year." My father's cousins, the children of Roberta and Vincenzo, lived out of state. What a shame they were missing out on this delectable polenta feast. I walked into the kitchen, kissed my dear Aunt Roberta, inhaled deeply the rich air of the kitchen. Ahhh! I felt so damned Italian I wanted to pinch everyone's cheeks!

In the next room, my eyes immediately ached from the darting whiplash of quick cut camera shots. MTV was on the TV. Foul-face teenaged niblets, curvaceous and yet anorexic, pouted and strutted, their bodies moist and dripping, sloe-eyed, their nipples popped out – I assume at the director's request. To no loss, I turned down the volume to hear what my 75-year-old great Aunt Roberta was saying from the kitchen.

"Okay," she shouted, waving a wooden spoon red with sauce, "Who's gonna go down in the basement and help Uncle Vincenzo stir the polenta?"

Though I loved them both dearly, and loved the tastes and traditions, I honestly preferred to get out of stirring. Polenta is a mushy Italian dish made from maize flour that must be stirred continuously over a stove for hours. It turns into an oozing plaster texture. Polenta is a tasty treat, but when it is traditionally made – all that stirring – it is exhausting, especially when you're used to modern conveniences. In fact, if someone does not figure out how to sell polenta in microwavable packages soon, all traces of this traditional Italian dish will vanish from the face of, well, at least America. Uncle Vincenzo, now going on seventy-nine, had always stirred the polenta. It was his baby. Just like how I always shucked the corn and my older sister Jewelia used to peel the onions. (But that was before she gave birth to her twins. Since then she doesn't do anything. Having babies not only robbed Jewelia of her childhood, it also sapped her spirit. My sister's given name is Julia, but she changed it when she turned 18 and got that job at the mall piercing ears.

Jewelia's twins already were six. She was only twenty-two. Jewelia slouched in the La-Z-Boy across the room, snapping gum, flipping absently through Auntie Roberta's Redbook magazine, her head bobbing to the high-voltage jangle that even I could hear from her stereo headphones. Just inches away from the TV sat her unblinking twins, those abysmal darlings she named Mary and Maria and who I called the "twin girls of a really different mother" – no one got my twist on

Warren Zevon – hoping that their diet of Pepsi, French fries and Zingers would not destroy the mental faculty that would someday allow them to understand my witty allusion. Jewelia quit piercing ears last year, opting for a better paying position as welfare mother. She moved into a trashy loft apartment where her boyfriend's thrash band practiced. Whenever her porky, undisciplined daughters visited our parents, they ran amok and jumped all over the couch. Jewelia never apologized, never made the kids apologize. She actually thought it was cute.

"I guess they want to be circus stars or something," Jewlia said as they bounced on Auntie Roberta's sofa.

"Hey, get down!" Auntie Roberta shouted. Jewelia gave Auntie Roberta a devil glare for being snippy with her children.

"How rude," Jewelia huffed. I could tell my sister thought her comment was uttered under her breath, but she never could judge the loudness of her own voice while listening to Metallica on her Walkman.

"Shut up, Jewelia," I said.

Auntie Roberta and Uncle Vincenzo had a beautiful home though it was kind of an awkward place because of the way they had added on to it like piecemeal through the years. A new bedroom here, a remodeled basement den there. The garage was once a rudimentary lean-to, a roof-on-stilts. Now it was heated and sheltered two cars and a workbench. Uncle Vincenzo built tables and chairs there, and just a few years back he added on a little greenhouse to grow vegetables year round. "Your uncle built it "higgledy-piggledy," she'd say.

It was full of the smells and sights of two people who lived together for over fifty years. The aura of food, the photographs of high school graduates of long ago, the wall full of anniversary portraits, taken every five years, where they gracefully aged in happiness and togetherness. I loved this house, with its faded scarlet rose-patterned carpet, the dozens of potted geraniums, the eerily comforting portraits of Christ.

I was only twenty, two years younger than Jewelia, but I tell you, worlds more mature, because there was no way I was going to repeat her mistakes. She got sloppy and careless with herself. She couldn't hold a job, smoked too much around her kids, and just scowled at the world, as if it were all of our faults that she lost at Russian roulette – in her game, the bullet being the persistent sperm that wriggled upstream like the defiant salmon. Her knockers drooped, her bottom swung with each step, and her eyes reflected her growing indifference. Worst of all was her venomous hatred of everything, which I know included herself. She got pregnant then gave up. She looked nowhere for inspiration. If she had at least tried just a little then I could love and respect her again and maybe even help. But she accepted nobody's advice. My parents and I tried to talk to her, suggest a job training program. We said it so sweetly. And even if we invited her to join us for ice cream, she'd get hysterical, telling us all to hell. "When you change a diaper," she told me, "then maybe I'll hear what you have to say."

So I no longer loved Jewelia. She walked through life making her own rules. She thought she was screwing over this unjust society by getting high all the time and not working anymore. I told her repeatedly that nobody gets rich on welfare, but she laughed in my face. (I could see her teeth were getting bad.) She let her kids walk through life without answering to anybody. What would Mary and Maria think when they grew old enough to realize that we must all answer for our deeds? I hope these poor unfortunate children did not damage our aunt and uncle's love seat.

"Keep your fat kids in line," I said.

"Now now," said Auntie Roberta, trying to douse the powder keg between me and my sister. She turned to Jewelia's daughters. "Want me to teach you how to play Cat's Cradle?" The twins looked at each other and rolled their eyes. Being identical twins, I'm sure they both imagined hearing the same laugh track responding to their hilarious responses to this silly doddering old goose holding the saucy wooden spoon. If I were Auntie Roberta I would've given each twin a wooden spoon whack across the face then turned the saucy utensil on their mother, that apoplectic speed metal bimbo who, unbeknownst to her and her horrid music, was just another digit, just another blip in the babies-having-babies broadening of the ignorant underclass in America. I brooded upon these thoughts till I heard the vibrant tenor of Uncle Vincenzo – or was it Tony Bennett – singing from the basement.

"You sigh a song begins, you speak and I hear violins...it's maaagic!"

Auntie Roberta smiled. Jewelia bobbed her head jerkily, her face twisted continually as she sloppily chewed bubble gum. Mary and Maria of course, being of like mind, shared an uncannily remarkable, identical sense of uncurious blankness. Oh, but hadn't they the nicest smiles?

"Hey Genie, how 'bout you? You help Uncle Vincenzo?" Auntie Roberta pointed the spoon at me. A dot of tomato sauce fell onto Jewelia's Def Leppard T-shirt.

"Shit, man!" Jeweled said. "Watch it, okay? Jeezus!"

Auntie Roberta shook her finger at Jewelia. "Don't talk like that here, young lady! And make sure the little ones don't play around my curtains." She stormed back into the kitchen crossing herself.

"I ain't even hungry," Jewelia said.

"Me neither," cried her daughters in unison.

"I'm stirring my arms off!" chanted Uncle Vincenzo from downstairs. "How 'bout some help from the youth of America?"

"I'll help him." I plodded down the stairs to the basement stove where Uncle Vincenzo cooked the polenta.

Even before the twins broke the arm off the rocking chair Uncle Vincenzo made, I expected this to be the last year we would be invited to their annual polenta dinner. I wanted to learn the correct way to make polenta – how often to stir, where to set the heat – any tricks Uncle Vincenzo was willing to share. I might even someday make it a family tradition of my own. Of course, to the exclusion of Jewelia.

My parents returned with strawberry frozen yogurt, which everyone liked except Jewelia. The twins flicked fingertip bits of polenta at Uncle Vincenzo's hunting beagle and ran around the table chasing the frightened dog. Everyone pretended to enjoy the meal except me. I stood and pounded the table like Vincent Gardenia in "Moonstruck," then turned to my sister.

"Not only do you have no respect for anyone, including yourself, you cannot even fathom the idea of respect. Come back, come back, come back Julia! Why have you given up? Don't you realize that the world is not lost just because you made a mistake? Think of it, think of the irony! The moment you gave birth, your own life ended. Doesn't that sound strange to you? Doesn't that sound like that is the exact opposite of what should happen? Shouldn't you now grow up instead of degenerate? Shouldn't you – more than me even – look up to people like...like...like our loving hosts, the kind and gentle and wise Auntie Roberta and Uncle Vincenzo? Don't they have things to tell you about keeping a home, raising your lovely daughters, perhaps even a few tips on how to maintain a love affair that could last more than six hours?"

I didn't really say that. I swallowed my thoughts and let them devour my insides. Instead, I turned to my sister and stared at her until she noticed.

"What?" she snapped.

"Shut up," I said.

People My Age

Henry Shaver rubbed his mother's shoulders but he felt like wrapping his fingers around her neck. His father was a bully and his mother let him do it. She let the bully breathe. She gave the bully nourishment. Henry was more like his father than he thought. He wanted to strangle the victim.

"Not so hard," Mrs. Shaver said.

"Sorry," said Henry.

Mrs. Shaver had a raspy cough. Henry stiffened. "Mom, you're sixty-six and you don't even have a doctor. Please, just go for a checkup."

"She doesn't need a checkup," Mr. Shaver said. "She needs rest and what she definitely does not need is aggravation from you."

He sat in a chair across the table but was leaning away from it, twiddling the bass dial on his hi-fi while an old Three Suns record played.

"Dad, I think the music's too loud. Mom's got a headache."

"Sshh," his mother said, gesturing for him not to upset his father. "Just keep rubbing my shoulders. That'll do me a world of good."

Henry continued the massage, careful to be gentle.

Mr. Shaver bit on his pipe and poured sugar into his coffee. The old man had retired five years before and each year his wife got sicker. He didn't have much to do. He spent a lot of time over her shoulder in the kitchen, criticizing her. He had been a dock foreman with a hawk eye for waste. But she didn't need to save time or cut corners. She wasn't pressed for time anymore. She had her own way of keeping a kitchen.

"That's the problem these days. Everybody running to the doctor for a sniffly nose. What a racket." Mr. Shaver's retirement mustache made him look like a small-time racketeer.

"It's more than a sniffle. She needs an annual checkup," said Henry. He was almost forty but still begging for a puppy. He was tense as a wet rope knot.

The Shavers had old world money worries, Great Depression worries. They had little respect for doctors. The old man was mildly diabetic and had a fibrillating heart, but he continued to eat donuts and bacon as a personal challenge to the world of medicine. In 1944, when he shook hands with General Patton, he decided that there was a part of him, too, that was Old Blood and Guts. Mr. Shaver had powerful forearms and wrists, tanned from over thirty years at the shipyard. He was smart and to the point. "You take too damn long to get to your point," he told Henry. "And these words you use – who even knows what they mean?"

"They pack a wallop for people who do," Henry said.

"But I don't," said his father. "So they're duds. They come out screaming from the plane hatch and go thunk in the mud. No ker-blooey."

"A checkup isn't a waste of time," said Henry. "It's preventative."

Mr. Shaver chuckled. "What you don't understand is that she doesn't have to go to the doctor to prevent something she doesn't have. These doctors like to prove they can find things that we can't."

"Doesn't her cough bother you?"

Mrs. Shaver turned sharply. "That's enough, Henry."

"Oh, okay, you're the devoted wife," said Henry with a sneer.

"Don't stir things up," she said. "If you're so concerned about our health, then don't get his heart going, please." To anyone listening, she sounded calm and gentle. To those who knew the Shavers, she was pleading.

Henry persisted. "What I'm saying is true. It's good advice. It's as if he doesn't care what happens to you!"

"Now I'm as tense as ever," his mother said. "My head is pounding."

"What is wrong with you?" Mr. Shaver said to his son. "You come through the door, her blood pressure goes up and she gets a headache and starts coughing. She doesn't cough half as much when you're not around."

"Why don't you just let me make you an appointment? The cough has been going on for weeks."

"Hush!" cried Mrs. Shaver. She winced from the headache. "The more you push this doctoring, the more I won't do it."

Selfish, Henry thought.

He took a glass of wine into the den and sat quietly in the dark room. Things he had built in high school shop class twenty years ago still adorned the walls. They were old, shelves and sconces, but polished with vigor. Mrs. Shaver was in the kitchen, rubbing her temples and coughing. Soon pots would clank and suds would swish and the sink would smell of lemon and grease. The accordion, bass and guitar of the Three Suns preserved the soundtrack of the house in 1952. His jaunty father entered the den and playfully popped Henry on the head with his rolled up newspaper. He turned on the light.

"Listen, Henry, I want to show you something. See that corner of the wall where the paint's bubbling? I'm going to have Ernie Burman tear down the plaster and put some insulation on the slate that's behind the bricks. The walls won't get so cold in the winter and so goddam baking hot in the summer. Then they'll repaint the walls and no more bubbling. What do you think?"

Henry's blood boiled. He couldn't stand looking at the wall that his father cared about more than, well anyway, he averted his gaze and looked out the window. Theodore Pappas sat on his porch next door, a black cigar in his mouth. He puffed white clouds and ran his hardened hands through his white hair. Henry jumped – his father had turned on the TV right in the middle of a baseball game and a loud crack of a bat, loud cheers and ecstatic play-by-play announcers.

"She's gone!" said Mr. Shaver. "That's a four bagger!" His stomach grumbled loudly. "Your mother's making us sausage sandwiches."

Henry wouldn't look at his father. He steadied his gaze out the window at the neighbor. "How's Theodore Pappas doing anyway?"

"He's okay. Keeping busy. He didn't make any wine this year," said Mr. Shaver.

"I mean, how is getting along without Mrs. Pappas," said Henry. "She got so sick so fast."

Mr. Shaver continued watching the game. "Look at that. It cleared eight rows, center field." He paused and added. "They couldn't catch it if they tried."

"No one even bothered," said Henry. "It was gone the second it left the bat."

Mr. Shaver said, "I mean Dina Pappas. Her cancer. It was pretty far along when they found it. What can you do?" Mr. Shaver shrugged.

"You nip it in the bud," said Henry. "If you don't, then it's you out there by yourself frying sausage, Dad."

"You better zip it, kid." Mr. Shaver pointed a menacing finger at his grown son. "Your sister never talks to us like that."

Henry Shaver left the house without eating dinner. He drove to the grocery store and bought a bottle of wine. He parked a block away from his parents' house, snuck up the alley and into Theodore Pappas' yard.

"Hi, Theodore!"

"Henry!" They embraced.

"My father said you didn't make wine this year." Henry gave Theodore Pappas the bottle.

"Thank you, Henry. Thank you so much. Oh, this is so nice. And your father and mother, they've been so good to me."

"They haven't been so good to themselves," Henry said.

"What do you mean?"

"My mom, she coughs, she gets sick. My father won't encourage her to see a doctor."

Theodore Pappas laughed. "People my age..."

He laughed some more, then removed the cork from the bottle with his Swiss army knife. Theodore took a long pull from the bottle and passed it to Henry.

"People my age," he said again, laughing so hard he had to take the cigar from his mouth.

Armand Hates Tea

Every night after dinner, Noney Lewis asked her husband the same thing. "Will you be joining me for tea tonight, Armand?"

Armand Lewis said no for forty-two years, the first one politely. For the next forty-one, he answered, "Stop asking me if I want tea already. I hate tea. Tea and toast, tea and jam, tea and crumpets. Any way you serve it – I hate it. To me, tea is best when it's in Boston Harbor. So no tea for me – thank you!"

The next night, after a delicious dinner of chicken paprikash and home fried potatoes, speckled with parsley from the Lewis garden, Noney rose and poured tap water into the kettle.

"Armand, will you be joining me for tea?"

Armand Lewis stomped out to the garage, propped a ladder against the brick wall, climbed onto the roof and sat there, perched at the peak, reading the newspaper, impaling coupons on the wrought iron rooster weather vane.

"Come down here," Noney said. "You're an old man. Your calcium is probably deficient. If you fall and break a leg, the bones will never knit and I'll be nursing you for the rest of your life."

"Yes," Armand answered, "forcing me to drink tea!"

Noney telephoned her son Larry, who lived five miles away. Larry put a client on hold and scribbled himself a memo to check into this Dad-on-the-Roof business.

"Come down, dear," Noney said to him calmly. He had been irritable lately. But not like this.

Armand ignored her and continued to read the funnies. "There's something fishy. Since Ernie Bushmiller died, Nancy is getting too clever."

Noney finally attempted to employ psychological persuasion on her husband. "Armand, you look handsome up there. The orange clouds behind you make you look like some statue of a god."

"There is no God," Armand announced. "For forty-two years, I've been saying no to your tea. Now, while I'm at it, I may as well tell you I will no longer attend Mass with you."

This was indeed a startling day for Noney Lewis. She never expected her husband to behave like this. She had to admit to herself that for all these years, she was well aware of Armand's disdain for tea. She should have chosen her words more carefully. But as for denying the existence of the creator, well, perhaps that was just displaced anger caused by Armand's squeaker defeat in the last church council election. Noney was enrolled in a continuing education course in human relations at the community college and, by God, she was enjoying it.

"What would Father Briden say, hearing you talk like that?" she asked.

"Father Briden's fruity!" Arnold said as he stood up on the peak of the garage.

"Heavens, don't jump."

"Jump? Who's going to jump? My legs are stiff. I'm stretching. And by the way, there is no heaven. There is no hell. There is no right and there is no wrong. Everything…just…is."

Noney wondered whether Armand was secretly taking a community college class, too.

"Your son is coming," she said.

"My son? Hah! That's no son of mine. Don't give me that look, Noney. Do you think I'm blind? I can see the resemblance."

"What are you talking about?" Noney pulled her sweater over the shoulders as the autumn evening whistled.

"Mattson," said Armand, folding the newspaper. "The milkman!"

"Mattson? Johnny Mattson?"

"And you thought I was an ignoramus."

"The milkman? Armand, he's been dead for twenty years."

"Good, the louse."

Noney didn't know what to say. It was true. During the late 1940s, at the height of suburban construction, Armand Lewis worked many fourteen-hour days in construction installing pipes in new neighborhoods. She was lonely.

She had lost her first son during World War II. The boy wasn't in the service. He was a three-year-old kid who had been swinging in a

rubber tire hanging from a tree in the backyard.
Some neighborhood teens, overzealous in their
patriotic search for scrap rubber, hastily snatched
the dangling tire and forgot to leave the boy
behind. He was never found again. But the
Lewises received a special Purple Heart from
President Roosevelt plus a visit from celebrity
Jerry Colonna, who personally delivered a tube
of Pepsodent toothpaste autographed by Bob
Hope and smeared with the lip prints of Hedy
Lamarr. Armand used the Purple Heart as a
sacred decoration on the robe of a statue of the
boy Christ, which was placed beneath the branch
where the tire once swung. Milkweed grew at the
statue's feet, an omen of subsequent things dairy.
In those days, Armand was a believer in many
more things.

Then came post-war sprawl, those damned
suburbs, the loneliness and then, when Noney
was at her lowest, along walked the
million-dollar smile of Johnny Mattson and his
promise of dairy at a discount, wink-wink.

"I never loved Johnny Mattson," she finally
said. "It's just that you were too busy laying pipe
in the suburbs."

"The only pipe being laid was at my house
while I was out working. Other guys came home
to loving wives and pot roast. I came home to a
wife with shifty eyes and an icebox full of
cheese. Just don't you worry about my calcium,
Noney. I've had enough calcium to bring a
mummy back to life."

"Larry's coming over," she said. "He thinks it's an emergency."

Armand sat down again. "Ah, that felt good. My knee was acting up. Damned trick knee. Noney, you're just like my knee."

"How is that?" she asked.

"Well, every once in a while, for no reason, you just go out on me." He looked around. "Our drain pipes are filthy. If we let these drain pipes go any longer, the whole garage will need bypass surgery." He tried to scowl at Noney. All she saw was a pout.

"Johnny Mattson," he muttered.

Noney leaned against an old oak tree. From Armand's unusual rooftop view, she was radiant, like an old Jackie Gleason mood music album cover. The darkening sky, the chestnut aroma of leaves on the wane and fallen summer seeds once again marrying the earth, these did not make Noney look younger, but instead made Armand think her more savory. Armand Lewis nearly lost his footing as his mind wandered back to the days of lush orchestras, tinkling jazz, laughter and steaks, martinis and Chesterfields.

And Johnny Mattson.

"So Larry thinks this is an emergency? An emergency? Listen, if Hitler would have choked on a chicken bone in '34, then there would have been no emergency, no war, right? And if you would've stopped offering me tea forty-one years ago, then I wouldn't be up here on the roof, stewing about the goddam milkman! It was an emergency long in the making."

"And if you hadn't been making the suburbs safe for chlorination, then I wouldn't have lain down with Johnny Mattson."

"Oh, so you laid down? That's a step up from the alleyway. At least you took him to the bedroom. Where did he leave the cheese, on my dresser?"

"Oh, Armand."

"Was it my fault people fled the cities?" Armand whispered in desperation. "Shush, here comes the baby milkman."

Noney tightened. "Swear to me you'll never mention this to him."

"We'll see."

There was nothing in the countenance of 38-year-old Larry Lewis to suggest he was bred from milkman lineage. He didn't look much like Armand either.

"Pop, what's going on?" Larry wobbled to the scene, loosening his tie, walking unevenly on the heels of his tasseled loafers, gulping air as if it were foreclosed property.

"I'm fine," Armand said, cleaning his ears with a match head. "I just noticed the gutters are filthy. In fact all the roofs in the neighborhood are starting to look shoddy. Ah, that's what happens when you get old. You can't keep up with your house. Pretty soon, the old neighbors drop like flies, the young couples buy the houses, fix the roofs. Nice roofs, but the hammering...who needs it? Me? I'm just checking the drain pipes and reading the paper. But it was nice to see you, Larry. Come back again anytime. Don't be a stranger."

"What are you sticking in your ear?" Noney asked.

"An Ohio Blue Tip wooden match. Why?"

"Don't stick a match in your ear," Larry said, adjusting his glasses, mopping his brow. "It's not safe. You shouldn't put anything in your ear smaller than your elbow."

"My elbows won't clean my ears."

"Come down here, Pop."

"Up yours, Mattson. I'm letting the match sulfur clean out my ear."

Larry squinted, hoping that would clear up the confusion. "What did he call me?"

Noney gulped. "He said *matches*, dear."

Minutes later, Armand Lewis climbed down the ladder. He assured his son that when the time came to clean the drain pipes, he would call a professional. Larry brightened. "I do taxes for some home repair guys. I'll give you their number."

"Do that," Armand said.

"How about a Coke?" Noney suggested. The sun winked over the horizon. "It's chilly out here," said Larry. "How about some tea?"

Noney glanced shyly at her husband. Armand raised his head and smiled. "Go ahead. I'm going to have a big glass of milk," he said, patting his wife on the bottom.

Rewind and Reflect

It came right after Kennedy was shot and just before the Beatles arrived and it went completely unknown by the press. A single condom fell out of my wallet and landed at my mother's feet. I remember her shock and the sound of her prattling to my father in her blue-nosed Eisenhower Italian.

To my parents, a wallet was for money – money earned by hard work and diligence and upright living. A rubber in a billfold was sacrilege, like cursing in church. Letting the condom fall out in front of my mother was more than just dumb. It was spiteful.

She told my father to do something, so he showed me his tool set.

"It's time you started one of your own," he said, and we spent the afternoon pricing wrenches. Back home, we fried some tomatoes and ate quietly in the kitchen. My mother was upstairs, still too ill to eat, too disgusted to cook for me. That night, as I lay restlessly in bed, she slunk into my bedroom like a specter.

Her voice trembled. "If you're thinking about this…fooling around business…well…don't."

The next day I felt so guilty I gave the condom to my pal in the high school camera club, Bobby Post, who made good money developing film that drug stores wouldn't.

When I look back at pictures of my childhood, I may as well be looking at pictures of dinosaurs. The world of my youth changed like a candle in the sun. After I became a father, I promised myself I would be more direct with my own son than my parents had been with me. So when my boy Chuck turned thirteen, I took him to Pizza Hut for The Talk.

My mother, God rest her soul, would never have approved of The Talk or of Pizza Hut for that matter. "You want pizza," she would have said, "Bring me flour, bring me cheese, bring up a jar of my sauce from the basement."

Chuck didn't appear to know what I was leading up to. He wolfed down four slices in minutes. I was too nervous to eat and rambled on about life and seasons and changing bodies and urges – unlike my mother's approach but just as bad – babbling on and on, saying nothing about everything. Chuck ate noisily so the booths around us couldn't eavesdrop. When I mentioned breasts, Chuck pushed his pizza away and rolled his eyes. I couldn't believe it. I thought I was cool by being so open, but Chuck's red face told me otherwise. He silently read the Pizza Hut story from the menu. The Talk was going nowhere, so I switched gears. "Chuck," I said, "it's time we got you a tool kit."

Chuck was never handy with tools, but suddenly he took an interest. As I sketched on a napkin to explain the difference between a regular and Phillips head screwdriver, he was ecstatic.

"Go on," he said loudly as he devoured another slice. "And don't forget to explain that metric stuff."

I suppose I was relieved, too. I kept talking about tools and that was that. It irked me for days that I never finished The Talk. My wife Delia told me not to worry, that Chuck had already heard it all on the Lifetime Channel.

"But I should be able to talk to him about sex."

Delia shook her head. "Fact is, he knows all about it. Face it, we didn't have cable in '65."

"Cable? Delia, men used to sweat and plant wheat and corn, father and son, side by side. We'd take to the woods with muskets and bring home meat. It was a rite of passage when a father let his son cut a pig's throat and hang his first kill in front of the smokehouse. Men stuck together in packs to ward off invaders from the villages down river. Now we sit in dens eating corn chips, unbuckling our pants and watching football."

"Why don't you two go fishing?"

"Too many mosquitoes." She agreed, remembering my horrible reaction to insect bites. Welts the size of silver dollar pancakes. In high school, I earned the yearbook honor to "most likely one day resemble a Japanese flag."

"I can't hunt, I can't fish, and now I can't even sit down in a chain pizza parlor and teach my son about life."

Delia smiled, calm and unconcerned. I was up all night in bed just thinking. In the other room I could hear the television cackle and groan and applaud and sell soap and insurance. That's it! I called Bobby Post.

We had stayed in touch since both our livelihoods depended on cameras. I worked as a Fotomat lab manager, and Bobby was a videographer. He captured the heart of any event – weddings, showers, bar mitzvahs, reunions, even births. Now I needed his help.

It was Memorial Day weekend and Bobby was busy taping family reunions and picnics, but he squeezed me into his schedule for a two hour session. I came home with a sparkling video production and handed the finished cassette to my son.

"What is it?" he asked.

"Just watch," I said and quickly disappeared around the corner to spy on him. Chuck popped the tape in. The production opened with Michelle Pfeiffer singing "Makin' Whoopee" from "The Fabulous Baker Boys." Then the scene dissolved to me trying to relax in a worn La-Z Boy recliner, which Bobby had placed in front of a backdrop of clouds and gulls. I was smiling awkwardly at a portrait that I held of my immigrant grandparents, Ima and Frank DeLuca. I faced the camera, stiff and double-chinned in my only suit and tried to be funny:

"Hi, Chuck. Boy that Michelle Pfeiffer sure has a pretty puh-face, huh?" At Bobby Post's advice, I allowed two seconds for laughter, which never came, then pointed to Ima and Frank DeLuca's plump and dour faces. "What I bet you didn't know is that 'Makin' Whoopee' was a popular song back when those two were known to make a bit of whoopee themselves. It just goes to show that love and a good love song are never out of date, huh?"

Chuck fingered the remote but kept watching. Meanwhile, on screen, I tried to explain what I knew about life: the importance of respect, the rewards of waiting for true love, the virtues of patience and kindness. I gave an awkward zucchini-and-condom demonstration. Chuck began to hum loudly.

I held up magazine ads of ladies' underwear and showed him a homemade Responsible Petting chart modeled on a baseball infield. Hunky-dory. But when I mentioned breasts, Chuck's humming revved like a mower.

Finally, I told the camera that after the tape ended I'd be available for questions in the kitchen. The production closed with a second from the film where Michelle Pfeiffer and Jeff Bridges argued – f-this and f-that -- just to let Chuck know that it wasn't all roses. I waited and waited at the kitchen table. There was no sound from the den. I waited half an hour, then finally looked into the den to see curtains blowing and an open window.

I didn't see Chuck for nearly a week, partly because I had to work double shifts developing Memorial Day pictures. Seeing all the snapshots of happy families, picnics and ball games broke my heart. All those waves and smiles and smart aleck curtsies. With each snapshot, my humiliation grew, as if they were saying, "Look at the fun we're having and you can't even talk to your son. You who lived through the sixties. For shame!"

I felt bitter that night. Again, Chuck wasn't home. "We're supposed to live in an era of openness," I said to Delia. "Why does he avoid me?"

"He's not avoiding you," she said. "He's just in love."

"In love?"

Delia laughed. "They just celebrated their anniversary. Two weeks."

"What? Two weeks? Whose anniversary?"

"You know the girl. Shawna Wallace."

I knew both Shawna and her parents, Bob and Paulene, who had just gone through a sticky divorce.

"A divorce-ridden neighborhood leads to devaluation of property," I said. Delia ignored me.

"Oh, you should see them. They've got the maddest crushes on each other," she said.

"She's from a broken home! Their house is probably unsupervised and unlocked. Just because Bob's advertising executive girlfriend wrecked his family, now they're leading my son down a tar pit hole of self-indulgence and self-destruction."

"I'm sure he watched your tape. He'll be okay."

"But he hasn't said a word to me."

"What do you want him to do? Give you an Emmy?"

I felt like a sitcom dad, the butt of jokes, a prime time eunuch. I waited and waited for Chuck to come home. He slipped quietly through the door just before eleven.

"Just what is this?" I said with feigned anger. Perhaps I did want that Emmy.

"Hi Dad," he said easily."

"Do you know what time it is?"

Chuck smiled. "I wasn't drinking, Dad. I wasn't in anyone's car."

"Were you with…Shawna?"

"Jeez, you say her name like she's a diseased goat. She lives two blocks away. What's the big deal?"

"Where have you been all this week, Chuck? Avoiding me?"

"How can I avoid you when you're always at work? I know I've been spending a lot of time with Shawna. But I like talking to her."

"Talking?" I said skeptically.

"Yeah, that's what we do. We talk."

"Just talk?" I raised my brow.

Chuck sighed.

"What did you think of that tape?" I asked.

Chuck turned as red as his grandmother once did. "Daaaaad! We talk!"

He ran out of the room, left the house early the next morning and was gone all day. When he came back that night, he left a videotape on my dresser and went into his room. I waited until his light went out then watched it.

The first scene was cloudy. Whoever held the camera was blowing smoke in front of the lens. Somewhere a stereo played fierce heavy metal guitar at a creeping speed. Next came Chuck's spiky hair, slowly emerging through the smoke. He said eerily into the camera: "Daaaaad...this is not a ghost....from the misty night....it's your son...Chuck...recognize me? I know I haven't seen you...in a week...but I assure you...I'm not really...a ghost."

Chuck then waved away the smoke, turned off the stereo and looked straight into the camera. It struck me how dark his eyes were.

"Dad, I know you're worried about me and Shawna, but don't worry. Shawna's folks both act real immature and play bitchy – excuse me, but there's no better word to use – phone games with each other and with Shawna, and if you saw how fed up Shawna is with both of them, you'd see how mature she is for her age, which is one year and four months older than me, but don't worry, because we're not doing anything, like, stupid. Okay, Greg, cut the smoke, man. So you see,

Dad, this isn't some fairy tale from the dark side. This is real. That's sort of all I have to say. And now, to fill up the rest of the tape, Greg will dub in some boxing highlights from his Sports Illustrated tapes. Oh, and Dad, Greg wasn't really smoking…"

"At least not technically inhaling," Greg added, off camera.

"Just special effects," said Chuck. "Thanks, and uh…uhm…uh…love ya, Dad."

I replayed that last part twice, then watched the boxing highlights. The next day I went into work to catch up on the final batch of holiday prints. I must have developed thousands of pictures, almost all from the holiday weekend: folks on vacations in boats; worried mothers clutching smiling toddlers near waterfalls; families waving from the mouths of caves; tourists with wind-whipped hair atop city skyscrapers; men holding beer cans and grilling chicken legs; rare belly shots of aunts reaching for a volleyball serve; grandmothers in kitchens hiding behind dish towels.

I loved them all. My little Fotomat lab chronicled America's private moments. These snapshots, I thought, will long outlast our petty troubles, and when our descendants find them in attic shoeboxes, they will be convinced that all went well, just as I always forget about my grandfather's thankless job in the mill and my grandmother's loss of three children to polio and pneumonia. I remember only the photo of them sitting happily in their garden, holding up jars of wine made from grapes crushes by the feet of the seven healthy children who survived. Love ya, Chuck had said to me, and all that next day his love rippled out into every photograph I developed and strengthened me.

Who Are We! (To Say What Stigmata with You)

> ***"Pete Townshend is God"***
> -graffiti

Test. Test. Can you hear me in the back?

Ladies and gentlemen, I don't know why they made John Lennon apologize. The Beatles themselves may not have been bigger than Jesus, but their music certainly turned out to be. They, themselves became the prelude, four John the Baptists, preparing us for the One, the Greatest, the Encore.

Like many of you, I was once all gone for Jesus. I just adored the pageantry of my St. Anthony's church, a fab place unto itself, especially in those waning days of the Latin mass, when every service seemed like a farewell tour. Learning how to genuflect and march in cadence to a First Holy Communion processional was as full of excitement and purpose as learning the Monkey or the Twist.

Once I was with my family on a long drive from Ohio to our vacation spot in sunny Florida. It was early Sunday morning and we were still hours away from our destination. Most kids would be anxious for the beach. Me? I worried that we'd be too late to make it to Mass at the church nearest our hotel. In one pocket rested my Roy Rogers wallet. In the other, my Daily Missalette. Oh, how I loved vacation church, where people wore colorful shirts and sang louder because they didn't know anybody. But it soon became clear that we wouldn't make it to our hotel in time to find a local church. So I pulled out my Missalette and officiated mass in the car. My older brother Roscoe groaned, but my devout father shushed him and even added sanctity by turning off the bustling I-95 to the more scenic Highway 1 where we could see God's green Atlantic. My father considered this body of water a miracle. "Listen to those waves, boys. You won't hear a lovelier chorus of angels than this."

There in the car I conducted mass. Later that afternoon, while playing on the beach in Titusville, I felt a pain in my left palm and ran to my mother. Mrs. Coriella, the woman who lived in a cottage all year around, took one look at my hand and clucked. "You touched a jellyfish. Don't ever touch those things, understand?"

Later, Roscoe poked me and laughed. "I know what you were touching. See what happens when you play with it. God punishes you." I wept, knowing that I had committed no sin. I was convinced that Mrs. Coriella and Roscoe were both wrong. This stinging in my hand was, without a doubt, stigmata. I suffered like Christ and became one with him.

Or so I thought. Three years later I was wearing Cuban heels and with my keen knowledge of guitar chords G, D and A, I won the hearts of my prettiest fellow eighth graders with my smooth medley of Twist and Shout, Glad All Over and Hippie Hippie Shake. Why, from a distance, you couldn't tell if I was a boy or a girl!

A few years later, after graduating to E and A minor chords, I watched The Who destroy their equipment on the Smother Brothers TV show. I was moved. Jesus turning over the money tables was chump change compared to this. BASH—DASH—CRASH—BOOM. I was a devout seventeen-year-old, but devoted to what? That weekend at St. Lucy's 11AM mass, my mind drifted and I imagined Father Briden finishing the service by bashing the gold cross into the vestibule and tossing out bright white communion disks to the first few rows while old Adeline DiGiacomo made the organ keys smoke.

Old friends of mine in the audience tonight must forgive me when I tell you that I lied. I never made it to Woodstock. I was one of those many thousands backed up on the New York state throughway. We heard about the concert on transistor radios. We tried to duplicate the spirit of the festival by passing the hat and giving the kitty to a guy on a motor scooter named Otto who promised to weave his way through the logjam and bring us back some mushrooms and Pabst. Well, we never saw Otto again. I consider that the ground zero moment of my generation's turn to conservatism. And in light of that, I'll give this to St. Lucy's church. At least when we put money in that collection basket each Sunday, we had the satisfaction of knowing that Father Briden would one day pepper his sermons with fascinating tales of his trips to Italy and Ireland.

Though my faith in all my fellow hippie washouts waned with each bad buzz and roommate who skipped out on rent, my fervor for the high power of the searing guitar never died. When I experienced see-me-feel-me-touch-me-heal-me, I felt the truth for the first time. I knew that Pete Townshend is God and that he spread his message through his speakers, big as my hometown water tower. I followed The Who around from concert to concert in 1969, lifting onto my shoulders girls from every American city with a concert hall. Just as I once knelt before a marble statue of the Man from Galilee, I now humbled myself in the presence of a larger power, right there onstage, whose guitar fingers bled so that I may hear the glory.

The beam of divine sunlight that once shone through the meadows of Zoalmont, Ohio onto the massive cross fixed atop St. Anthony's steeple, a scene that made my knees buckle and tears spring from my eyes, that that was just an opening band compared to the laser lights blasting out like an illuminated octopus from the stage where Pete hopped to the ditzy-beady-festive-gypsy part of "Baba O'Reilly." The divine light shone not from the sun, a mere self-luminous gaseous sphere, but from the stage where there stood He who offered salvation to the teenage wasteland.

1969. 1970. 1971. And so it went, year after year, until by the late seventies I walked around high on the knowledge that I had eternal salvation and I carried my portable stereo with me everywhere to share Pete's word with all. Not everyone appreciated my ministry, although I think the fellow who kicked in my speakers has more in common with Pete than he thinks. I never hated such people, always tolerated their abuses. Perhaps I was so tolerant of these modern Philistines because I could barely hear them. Yes, I spent the seventies losing much of my hearing. It discouraged me for a while until I read that Pete, too, suffered from partial deafness. Imagine, I suffered the same wounds as Pete Townshend. For the second time in my life, I felt a calling from above, only this time it was for real. Stigmata!

At first I thought I was alone, the sole human chosen by God to suffer Pete's wounds and carry on his work. But soon I found comfort in all of you, this mighty legion of fellow followers who have also suffered this same stigmata. We have all felt the jolt that called together m-m-m-m-my generation!

And we join together to reinforce our strength. Because there is temptation out there. Just last week, a good friend of mine, an Elvis worshipper, tried coaxing me into the fold by waving in my face a Doritos salad with a Percodan garnish. My own cousin cannot lie down with her husband unless he wears around his neck the scarf thrown to her from the stage by Tom Jones twenty-one years ago. Not to mention the woman who worships Ben & Jerry because she suffers ice cream headaches.

But ladies and gentlemen, we won't be fooled again! He said, "Let my love open the door!" And we shall – what? What's that? Oh. We shall turn up the volume and start again for those of you who couldn't hear.

Afternoon Surprise

The theme music faded, and the first words
spoken by Leeza Jessie Jones were
uncharacteristically somber. She looked into the
camera, which had been equipped with a special
lens to catch the glistening in her eyes like
diamonds.

"Our hearts go out to our guests, Lillian and
Michael Meeker. They are the parents of a
missing child. We thank them for coming and
today we hope to understand more about their
tragic story."

The Meekers bowed their heads humbly. The
audience clapped respectfully. Lillian Meeker
explained how Krista, their six-year-old daughter,
had wandered away at the mall. Michael Meeker
said the police investigations met dead ends.
Next, a psychologist appeared to discuss the
horrible strains on the marriage that Lillian and
Michael Meeker had to withstand and offered
some statistics about missing children.

Leeza Jessie Jones bit her lips in a way that
would make Bill Clinton videotape and study it.
In a heartbreaking moment, Lillian Meeker
bravely told the audience, "It feels like someone
just reached into my chest and tore out my heart.
Somehow, and I don't know how, I will have to
move on and face life. Please, please…all of

you..don't ever let your children out of your sight. If I only knew where she was…"

"Let's hope we can do something about that," said Leeza Jessie Jones. She then introduced a psychic named Quentin Leep, a specialist in finding missing people. He had a proven record tracking down runaway teens, deadbeat dads, and people living incognito in trailers avoiding big captain gains taxes. Quentin Leep spoke with closed eyes while he fiddled with a deck of playing cards.

"Your daughter is very close to you," Quentin Leep told the Meekers.

"She'll always be close to us," said the father. "I don't go a minute without thinking about her."

"She remains close to you," said Quentin Leep, eyes still closed.

Lillian buried her face in her palms and her shoulders shook. Michael comforted her.

Leeza Jessie Jones smiled wryly. "We'll find out how much closer…when we come back from this break."

The Meekers raised their heads, befuddled.

After the commercial, Leeza Jessie Jones probed Quentin Leep.

"You say that you feel the missing girl is close?"

"Yes, Leeza, I'm getting a very strong feeling about that. I'm feeling red, which is a very strong, close color."

"I know when I wear a red dress my boyfriend likes to get strong and close," said Leeza.

The audience laughed. A few hooted. Lillian and Michael clutched each other's hands.

"What would you say to your daughter if she was right here with you?" said Leeza Jessie Jones softly, her eyes darting from the Meekers to her floor director and back.

Michael Meeker's chin quivered as he spoke. "I would tell her…that we love her…and we're sorry…and…" but he could not continue. Audience members wiped their eyes with tissues provided by the show's sponsors. Leeza Jessie Jones leaned over and patted the Meekers' shoulders.

"We have a little surprise for the Meekers," she said.

A recording of "Rubber Duckie" played – the missing girl's favorite song – as Leeza Jesse Jones pointed to the curtain and said, "Please welcome to our show, the missing little girl, Krista Meeker!"

Now seven, wearing a brand new red outfit provided by another sponsor, the girl appeared hesitantly from behind the curtain. Michael Meeker's eyes widened. Lillian Meeker took quick shallow breaths and her hands shook. They were numb, frozen to their chairs.

Leeza Jessie Jones' smile was big as a quarter moon in a cloudless sky. She poked the parents playfully on the shoulders. "Go ahead, go see Krista," she said. "It's really, really her."

The audience caught on and erupted in wild cheers, chanting "Kris-ta, Kris-ta, Kris-ta!" The host gently led Krista Meeker to her parents and the family finally embraced.

"When we called you three weeks ago to appear on this show, did you have any idea this would happen?" Leeza Jessie Jones asked.

Michael and Lillian stammered incoherently. Leeza saved the day by holding out her hand and saying, "Ladies and gentlemen, the Meekers have been reunited. They not only have each other, they have some brand new prizes we'll give them right after this break!"

After the commercial break, Leeza took questions and comments from the audience.

"I'm really happy for the parents that they got their little girl back," said one tall woman with her hand on her hip. "But at first they didn't even hug her. There's something weird about that."

"I just want to know why, you know, this lady is not watching her daughter at the mall?" said a young man with a backwards baseball cap.

"I have a question for the little girl. Did you run away from home because of abuse?" asked a woman in a blazer who added an extra syllable to every word she spoke. A middle-aged man asked Quentin Leep to predict stock futures. Quentin Leep then spent the rest of the program describing the laws of insider trading and why, because of his clairvoyant gift, he was not allowed to discuss the stock market with anyone.

Meanwhile Michael and Lillian Meeker were getting on-air makeovers.

Hunting Down the Burglar

The last time Camille and I were together as husband and wife, she behaved like a raving maniac. She'd seen too many Joan Crawford movies. She swept her hand across my desk, letting papers fly. She cried, "Is love here? Is there love in this pie chart? Does love even make the tiniest sliver?"

I bundled up my reports and went to my office. It was one a.m.

Typically, at work, appointments lined up outside my door and around the corner. Camille should have made an appointment.

They say that a beautiful thing in life is watching your lover sleep. That, I gave Camille. She came home to recorded messages that I'd be late. Then I'd straggle home beat, peel off my suit, and as if that suit were my backbone, I'd fold up onto the sofa. I looked and sounded like a junk store accordion. That's how she described me. Not such a beautiful thing I guess.

Camille wanted a home and a baby. I couldn't indulge her. I had a mistress – work. One had to go and so went Camille. Neither made me happy but I gave the chance to Work.

Camille was beautiful. But after a time I really didn't know her anymore. I was left only with her beauty and her dissatisfaction, which turned her beauty sour. I don't know why, but one with soured beauty is easy to hate. Maybe movie magazines teach us that.

Each morning Camille woke up next to a stranger. Then one day, I woke up alone. I went directly to work.

I do wonder how she is. She is probably happy. She could be dead. If anything happened, I'm sure someone would track me down. What if a stranger knocked on my door and said, "Your ex-wife is dead." Would my jaw drop? Would I cry, "Oh, my God!" I'd probably say, "How did you find me?" So, do I really wonder how she is? Sometimes.

I left them both, my wife and my job. Count that two divorces. Now I'm rested and content. Camille would doubt that because I still only work and sleep. She would say I am only rested. But now my work requires no neckties or business lunches. Now I get paid to whistle in the dark.

Long ago, I paid more money for a wallet than I now earn in a two-week paycheck. Now I don't even carry a wallet. I've lost too many to anemic creeps with dull knives. At Goodwill I found a paperback that fits in my back pocket and that's where I keep my cash. In my neighborhood the thieves don't read.

For a long time, I thought the book was about Christmas, about Jack Frost, wintertime, sleigh rides. Once I pulled it out to pay for a hamburger and took another look. It was Robert Frost.

The book always opens to page 94, a poem called "Mending Wall." Usually I read it on the toilet. I've read "Mending Wall" about twenty times, but I just let my eyes drift over the words. I never thought about "Mending Wall" until that afternoon when I last saw Melvin Dimes.

Melvin Dimes came out of his room twice a day and stood on the rickety fire escape overlooking Chalk Boulevard to wave at school buses that passed beneath him. Once they passed, Melvin would go back to 17-B, a den of foulness. Once, he closed his door and a thin orange piece of onion skin blew down the hallway like tumbleweed. Melvin was strong as a crane and just as ugly. He creaked and grunted and groaned through the halls of the Raven Hotel, giving off his crane steam, a lanky machine in need of oil.

Why did he bother shaving? He missed such big patches of his beard. His face resembled aerial topography photos. Sweat blackened the creases of his weathered skin, looking like rivers viewed from a mountaintop. He was about seventy-five, maybe more, and walked with a powerful bounce. He carried brown bags full of instant pudding boxes and potato skins to the dumpster every couple of days.

I'm in 22-B. My window overlooks Chalk Boulevard. I see too much broken glass out there. Hardworking people rub their aching backs but keep on with their convenience stores, pawnshops, chicken wing shacks and the last remaining deli. The sun doesn't shine much here, but when it does, God keeps the Vitamin D for other neighborhoods. There is a still decent music store up the street where kids carry guitars and horns and flutes. When I hear the scales of a trumpet from the chubby kid waiting for his bus, I think of how grand this neighborhood once was, back when the marble seraphim lining the Raven entrance welcomed guests with beacon calls. Now the marble is cracked, noses and legs gone, trumpets chipped into kazoos. And with all that broken glass on the sidewalk, the neighborhood looks out of control.

I've never seen a kid on the school bus look up at Melvin Dimes, let alone wave back. For that matter, I've said little to Melvin Dimes and we've lived a few doors away from each other for seven years. We don't bring new neighbors Bundt cakes. No one exchanges recipes. We warn each other where not to walk past nine. I see Melvin in the afternoons. Every few weeks, in the hall on my way to work, I say hiya. I work nights guarding a storage garage. People pay good money to lock up stuff no crook I know would even sniff at – ugly sweaters, awful record albums, boxes of mismatched spoons and forks. When I go to bed, Melvin Dimes is waving to the morning buses. When I wake up and fix a can of something to eat, Melvin Dimes is waving to the afternoon buses.

Not long ago I was sitting on the toilet. I'd been there about five minutes – the tenant handbook entitles us to ten – reading page 94 when all of a sudden I heard Melvin Dimes sobbing out in the hall.

"Come on, Melvin, I've got five more minutes."

But he kept crying.

"What's up, Melvin?"

This could be an old-man's-bowels emergency, so I yanked up my pants and opened the door. Melvin just stood there, looking around at everywhere but me.

"It's all yours," I said, but Melvin wouldn't budge. He stood still and numb as a rock. I heard sirens squealing, trucks honking, buses screeching and Melvin Dimes sniffling. His eyes were sunken and red, his jaw hung loose. In that dim hallway, he could've been made of wax.

"You don't want to use the can?" I asked.

He moved toward me. His chin bobbed up and down.

"Come on, Melvin, let's go have some coffee." I'm really not this sociable, but he was moving so close to me, I had to say something. So I took him to my room.

No one had seen my room since that dancer spent the night, Marcia, her onstage name was Marquette, or something French, and that was nine months ago. I hadn't cleaned up since so I picked up a few shirts to give Melvin a place to sit. He whimpered like a pup and held his arms out. My Lord, he wanted me to hold him! Think quick, I told myself, and so I put a cup in his hands. I heated water on the hot plate and soon we were sipping instant coffee.

I tried to loosen him up. "Why didn't you use the bathroom, Melvin? That's why I got out so quick. You could've had your ten minutes plus five of mine."

Marvin gulped for air. "If I'd gone in, I'd have killed myself."

"Did I stink it up that bad?"

"Oh no, I wasn't saying that."

"I know, Melvin. I was just joking. It's okay. Calm down."

"I don't understand jokes anymore. I just want to die. Take me down to the cemetery, will you? Maybe I'll just fall into a hole."

He grabbed his stomach and bent over, wet with tears and tension. He tried nobly to contain himself, but it spilled out in coughs and cries. I tossed him a towel. "Wipe your face. The towel's dirty already so don't worry about messing it." He blew his nose and mumbled. I stared at the clock, fidgeting, and soon my nervous fingers were around my book.

"Melvin, listen to this. Melvin, you listening?" I started reading the poem. "See? It's called 'Mending Wall' by Robert Frost."

Melvin leaned close to the book and squinted. "Please don't read no love poems. I just couldn't bear no love poem."

"This isn't a love poem, Melvin. This is about Robert Frost and his farmer neighbor. They're fixing a stone wall that borders their properties. Frost wonders why the hell they need a wall since he's got apple orchards and the neighbor's got pine trees. How come we need a fence, Frost says to the neighbor. The neighbor, he's stubborn, and just says, *good fences make good neighbors*, just like his daddy said before him. And that's that. Makes you think, doesn't it, Melvin? Especially with you and me being neighbors."

Melvin burst into tears. Dammit! I'd gone blue talking fences and for what?

I said, "What we need here is good fences and thicker walls and our own damn bathrooms!" Though I tried to be angry, I wasn't. In fact, I could just picture walking up and down a fence, fixing her up, with Melvin Dimes on the other side, lifting stones in the bright sunshine and clean air, listening to birds, flicking away June bugs, taking a hearty piss in the stream. Here we had nothing but onion skins, broken glass and ten minutes in the toilet.

"Melvin, you need money? I got a little money."

Without looking up, he nodded no. He cried quietly but it came out steadily, like he'd never cried before, not once in his life, and now it just poured and poured. His tears smelled ancient, like vinegar left behind in a summer cottage. He reached into his pocket and handed me a crumpled newspaper page. It was worn and rubbed thin but was only from yesterday's edition, the obituary of Audrey Whiting, eighty-one, a retired schoolteacher, never married, garden club, literacy council. When she turned eighty, four hundred former students and colleagues honored her at a banquet.

"Did you go to this dinner?" I asked.

"No."

Why not, I wondered. "Didn't she know you loved her?" How those words came out of my mouth I'll never know. Melvin cracked his knuckles.

"She didn't know me. She spoke to me once. She asked me…no, she told me…to turn up the heat in her classroom. She said, *we'll be in the Depression forever if these children aren't warm enough to do their times tables.* She said that on January 23, 1937, fourth period, right before lunch."

Melvin eyed the fifth of whiskey I kept on the table.

"Pour some," I said, holding out my cup, too. He nipped our coffees.

"Yes, Miss Whiting said, *turn up the heat, the ink is freezing!* on January 23, 1937, fourth period, right before lunch."

The first taste of whiskey lifted a bit of Melvin's burden.

"Things pass," he said. "I haven't thought about her for years. Back then, though, oh, what a flaming torch I carried, hot as the furnace I shoveled coal into each day. But the fire went out, they all do. And yet I kept shoveling. I kept my back strong and my heart healthy. For what? I don't know."

He turned and for the first time looked directly at me.

"Take me down to the cemetery."

"Where she's buried?"

"Not for her. For me. Take me to the cemetery. I want to die."

"Come on, Melvin."

"I'd forgotten her, but seeing this made me remember that I once loved her. I loved her! Oh, what a glorious feeling!"

"Even if she didn't love you back?"

"Are you trying to make me feel worse? Well you can't. I can't feel worse than this, kid. You give me cheap coffee and cheaper whiskey, but it's still better than what I've got down there." He nodded toward his room. "And I thank you. You're trying to be nice, but you still think I'm an old idiot."

Then Melvin turned harsh. "Miss Whiting! I'm sure she thought I was just a big ugly baboon who walked bowlegged and swept floors and fixed flats on the buses and gave cigarettes to kids who grew up to be crooks and councilmen. No, I didn't just get ugly in old age. Even then I didn't have no front teeth. My boarding house didn't have no bathtub. I rubbed garlic on my chest each morning and to this day I don't get sick. Now I'm stronger than any of those stone fences you talk about that keep falling apart and need fixing. I have my health, but I must have my health. I cannot get sick! Who will say *God bless you, Melvin* when I sneeze? To be alone and sick is getting sick twice as bad. Life is a curse!"

Melvin brooded. I swallowed nervously. I desperately wanted to say something. I held up my glass. "How about a toast?"

194

"A toast? What the hell for? She's dead and I'm old and unloved. Are you outta your mind?"

Then Melvin's voice softened as he kept speaking.

"I hated that job, too, hated it. Except for every morning, just knowing I'd pass Miss Whiting in the hall. Folks said she smelled like lilacs. I doubt if her mother rubbed her down with garlic. It was such a relief to sleep because every waking moment just shook, pounded, with the thought of Miss Whiting."

"Now I can't remember her face. Or her lips. Her fingers, her hair, her eyes, nothing, none of the things I cherished in all my waking and dreaming hours. All I can remember now is the sound of her footsteps in the empty hallways after school. The echo of her little rabbit high-heeled steps on her way to the bus out back. Clippety-clippety, every day, right past my boiler room. I listened every day and not once did they stop, or even slow down to wish me a good night."

"Melvin, drink your coffee. Finish the bottle if you want. I have to go to work." Before I left, I tuned my little radio to a big band station. There was some jazzy clarinet playing. "Say, Melvin, do you know who this is playing?"

"Is this Junior High Quiz?" he said with a sneer.

Stew in your own broth, I thought, and went to work.

In the moments before dawn I returned home to find my door wide open. I didn't own much of value, but what I had was gone. Roz in 26-B said she saw Melvin Dimes leaving at 2 a.m. with three shopping bags. The only thing gone from his room was his clothes, just a few old flannel shirts.

He left Audrey Whiting's obituary on my pillow.

The manager said Melvin had lived here for twenty-three years. Imagine leaving a home of twenty-three years for a hot plate, a radio, a watch and three hundred in cash. The Raven Hotel isn't much, but just like you've got to believe in God just so you won't go crazy, you've got to hang your hat even in the lowliest places to call something home. Even the sons of the most worthless mothers get a lump in their throats on Mother's Day.

Two weeks passed and they finally rented 17-B to, of all people, a dancer. I keep my distance.

I put the obituary in my book. I can tell you right now without looking, it's on page 94. The obituary makes me think. No matter how fast and long we run, the ghosts are faster. Once the ghost catches up, he puts a spell on us, makes us a steel-eyed vigilante who goes fearlessly into the night to kill the burglar and take back what was stolen from us.

There are times when I forget what Camille looked like. How could I forget that beauty which consumed me? I fell in love with her from the first moment I saw her. I decided to love her, to sweep her off her feet, to convince her that I was the very best thing that could ever happen to her. All this without knowing who she was. All this without hearing her voice. All this without her knowing it.

When I hear high heels on a hard floor, I think of her. Though I still can't remember what she looks like, I whisper her name. *Camille.*

All this broken glass infuriates me. I complain about it to the cops who patrol the neighborhood. They laugh and tell me to lighten up, so I do. I tell them that the broken glass resembles a coral reef when the three o'clock sun hits it from the side.

There I sit at my window, waiting for the school buses. Something tells me that one of those kids keeps looking up at the fire escape.

Make the Call

Three young men sat in the back of the
pick-up truck in the A&P parking lot. They
swung their legs, chugged Coke from plastic
2-liter bottles and smoked. They shouted over the
Lynyrd Skynyrd tape blasting from the truck
stereo. The last grocery shoppers of the night
snuck looks at the boys, cringed at the noise, and
drove off the lot faster than usual.

The A&P closed. Half of the parking lot lights
went off. The clerks and cashiers drove off or got
picked up.

The store manager, Wilson Perkins, and Louis
Brimi, a very capable high school senior who
was the night manager of the produce
department, closed up and walked out together
across the dimly lit parking lot.

Louis Brimi sighed at the sound of the noisy
truck, but unless his boss was going to say
something about it, he would ignore it.

Wilson Perkins was a slight, nervous man who
got along well with the ladies who shopped at his
store. Louis Brimi's father once told his son that
Wilson Perkins was born to run a grocery store,
that he loved darting from aisle to aisle like Mr.

Whipple telling old ladies how to shop.

Those same ladies had been complaining to Perkins about the noisy truck radio and how these boys were loud and vulgar. Margaret Nicotera asked Wilson Perkins what he was going to do about it. Sweat beaded up on his red face and he stammered.

"Well...are they being, as you say, vulgar, toward you?"

"Not me, exactly," she said. "Just potty mouthing the whole town."

"But not directly to you, correct, Mrs. Nicotera?"

"Them boys don't even know I'm alive. But do we really need to hear that talk, Mr. Perkins?"

"Well...I'm having a sale," Perkins said to the ladies. Louis Brimi watched Perkins' eyes shift and his pointy overbite bounce up and down nervously over his lower lip. "Thirty percent off all meats!"

"Everything?" They squealed with excitement.

"Yes indeed, all meat. Sirloin. Prime rib. Roast."

Louis Brimi knew there was a sale on hamburger. That's it. But a sale on all meat? Perkins was on the ropes.

Louis Brimi had been taught by his father to work hard, to speak calmly, to think things through rationally. His father ran a barbershop. The barbershop. There were hairdressers and hair stylists, but after Charley Kennedy retired, Tony Brimi became the last barber. Louis was on his way to pick up his father at the shop downtown.

From there they were going straight home to await the truck from the vineyard. Tonight they would receive their load of grapes. Louis Brimi looked forward to crushing and pressing the grapes. He had not always relished wine making. All through his childhood he detested the day. He'd much rather be out jumping into piles of leaves or playing football in the mud. Instead he helped his father press grapes.

Then his grandfather Louis died. Little Louis all of a sudden found a deeper meaning in the crushing of the grapes, the bursting of the skin, the juice set free, the barrel filled. Working in the grocery store changed his view as well. The vegetables he weighed and priced were the same his grandfather and father picked freely from their backyard gardens. Every time Louis Brimi saw a customer read a wine label, he remembered his grandfather and father holding small jelly jars of their own wine up to the light to see if the sediment had settled. If it was clear, it was ready to drink. If not, they'd wait. Simple as that. Wine customers knew nothing of squeezing, stirring, straining, holding small glasses up to a bare basement bulb.

One year, long before Louis was born, his grandfather said, "God make-a the grape and man make-a the wine." By the time Louis came along, this was something they all said – every year – to kick off the moment when the first grape was crushed.

"Man make the wine," Louis Brimi whispered to himself as he jingled his car keys in the A&P parking lot.

The truck stereo got louder.

Wilson Perkins shuddered. "Do you think you could tell your friends to turn down their music, Lou?"

Louis Brimi closed his eyes. Not again, he thought.

The guys sat on the flatbed of the truck.

"Hey Lou," said Clint Ligget, the boy who drove the truck.

"Hard day at work?" laughed Tim Fox, the dirty, black-eyed small boy who sat in the middle. His laugh turned into a cough.

"Bet he worked a helluva lot harder 'n you ever did," said the third boy, Chris Binzik, shoving Tim Fox's shoulder.

Everybody liked Louis Brimi, a straight-laced boy with a good sense of humor. They admired the way he played guitar at school talent shows, though the guys weren't crazy about the ballads Louis played, they envied the hot chicks he accompanied while they sang.

Louis Brimi smiled.

"Got a match?" said Tim Fox.

Louis Brimi went through the motions of tapping his pockets. "Nope, sorry."

"Why do you need a match?" said Clint Ligget. "There's a lighter in my truck."

"Yeah, and I got matches, butthead," said Chris Biznik, flicking hair from his eyes. Tim Fox spat onto the ground.

"I wasn't asking you guys," said Tim Fox. "I'm asking him." He popped a Marlboro to his lips. He pointed to Wilson Perkins, who had kept on walking toward his home, which was four blocks away.

"Hey, I'm talking to you!"

Louis Brimi gave the other two boys a hey-help-me-out look.

They tried to calm down the short hothead. "Come on, Fox!" said Chris Binzik.

Clint Liggett just laughed and swatted Tim Fox and said, "Pick on someone your own size – like a first grader!"

Tim Fox pushed them away, pulled a pint of vodka from his jacket, pulled down the final swig and flung the bottle to the pavement.

The grocery store manager lurched, stopped and turned. He took a deep breath, so noticeable that all three boys on the truck bed laughed and mocked his sigh. In the darkness Louis heard Wilson Perkins mumbling something. Had there been more light, he would have seen his boss shaking, his buck teeth bobbing.

"Man, you're nervous," Tim Fox said. He hopped off the truck and walked toward the man. Perkins' eyes widened. "I just wanted a light."

Louis Brimi turned to the other boys. He knew them all from school, but they took different classes. By now they were not trying to stop their friend. They were bored and drunk, too.

"Turn the music down, fellows," said Wilson Perkins.

"I asked you a question," Tim Fox said with a mixture of menace and playfulness. He stood six inches shorter than Wilson Perkins, and thirty years younger. "You...got...a...light?"

Wilson Perkins shook then stiffened. Louis attempted diplomacy.

"Guys...guys...all we're saying is how 'bout you keep the music down out there?" Louis said.

With that Chris Binzik stepped down, took a few steps to the driver's side, reached in and cranked the volume up higher.

Louis Brimi exhaled through his nose and peered off at the night sky. The half moon, the smattering of twinkling stars all made this feel so small. What did bad, loud music or a grocery store mean when you looked up at the vast universe, the maker of the grape?

Louis Brimi finally looked down when he heard his classmates chicken clucking as Wilson Perkins walked away. Louis turned toward his own car. His classmates said nothing more.

That night, Louis and his father talked about what happened as they rinsed the grapes in a barrel in the driveway.

"When you don't got anything to keep you busy, when you don't know who you are, that screws up nature," said the barber to his son. "Animals prey upon the weak, yes, because they are hungry. These guys prey on the weak even when they're not hungry. That throws off everything."

Louis Brimi thought about that. The next day at work, the same three boys sat perched on the gate of the truck, their music getting louder and louder as the moon rose. Louis carried out groceries. They laughed like donkeys when an empty bottle tossed from one boy to the next slipped through butter fingers and smashed on the ground. They flung hair out of their eyes and gulped at 7-11 cups filled with whiskey and Coke. They smoked and howled like wolves at ladies old enough to remember World War I. Customers and employees alike complained to Wilson Perkins. Do something about it, they demanded.

Wilson Perkins retreated to his office. Louis knocked and entered. Wilson sat at his desk, eyes focused on an open binder. Louis had seen him in this position a hundred times. Only today, Wilson's shoulders shook and he wept, squeaking and panting.

"If you don't want to kick them out, then call the cops!"

Wilson Perkins gulped. He looked at Louis Brimi.

"Could you?" said Wilson Perkins.

The Not Knowing

Spooky Perry got his name when he was seven. He picked a cayenne pepper from his grandfather's garden and said, "If we mere mortals could harness the energy that nature has trapped in these membranes, then and only then can we understand the almighty power of God."

The entire 4th of July picnic froze.

"Spooky," his aunt finally said.

I think it's poetic, although it's not technically poetry because Spooky drives a bread delivery truck and he doesn't write down his unique thoughts. "Can't write while I drive," he says. If he could, though, he'd be a poet.

Once he said to me, "Sherri, you got hair that glows like a bonfire on homecoming night."

Spooky sat with me on the hillside at the south end of the park. Not a city park. Trailers. Mobile homes, I should say, though if you're going to change the name from trailer park to something else, mobile home village isn't much more than lipstick on a pig. Anyhow, I see as many pigpens in pricey developments as I do in my trailer park. So when the nights were especially dark, me and Spooky would watch the town's lights flick off one by one. We'd try to guess exactly which house was turning in. Then I'd lie in his arms like a baby and he'd say, "Look at that sliver of moon poking its nose around the corner of the cloud." Or, "Listen to those owls. Hey, owls, I got just one thing to say back to you: *Guess who!*"

Anyway, he is a poet.

Those owls were once my own personal chorus and I was their goddess. But that was then. Now the owls are just loud, like a teenager's boom box or a snoring husband, only I can't call the police or poke anyone in the ribs.

I cut hair at Willa's, right off the freeway exit. Willa had the vision, and a few township trustee connections, back in the sixties when she built the place. Within a year, Route 11 was built. Downtown Zoalmont is dead, but Willa's is booming. There are many fine gentlemen zipping up and down Route 11 on business from Cleveland and Youngstown to Steubenville and Pittsburgh and West Virginia and beyond. They all need haircuts and love getting them on company time. They've been saying lately, "Sherri, you look tired." Well, I am tired, but I haven't missed a birthday yet. I've got a box of cards marked with my customers' birthdays and on the day they come in nearest their birthday I knock off ten percent and give them a cupcake I freeze in big batches in the back. Willa doesn't eat that ten percent, I do. Willa doesn't make those cupcakes. I'll just stop there before you think I'm patting myself on the back. But I will congratulate myself on the quality of my friends.

I sure can pick them. I love chit-chatting while I clip their hair but I like talking to more than just the backs of heads. That's why I invited them out to the house. I've seen enough roots and scalps. Let me see their eyes.

Everett Wooster has clear blue eyes. He always says, "Sherri, you know our time together isn't complete without Patsy." So I put on some Patsy Cline and we dance to "Back in Baby's Arms." Everett is fifty-five-ish with long gray pork chop sideburns and a spark to his smile that could light a blowtorch. His wife's name was Patsy, too, and she died way too young from Lou Gehrig's a few years before I got to know him. Folks say Everett stuck by Patsy with a dog's devotion and I can feel the depth of his loyalty when we dance. Two people dancing in a trailer without knocking over anything, there's some magic in that. "If I break it, I'll buy it," Everett said, and he's never owed me a cent. He once said, "Diseases like Patsy's make folks lose faith in God. Not me. I know there's a heaven because there's no way a woman like my Patsy could've died like she did without comfort and luxury waiting for her in the next world."

I always have a good clean cry when Everett leaves and if he hadn't vowed to never remarry I'd have thrown a net over his head long ago.

I bought a junky guitar at Thrift City for when Dave Pennington comes over. He's a high school senior ready to pull open the curtain on life. When the rest of the kids listen to music that sounds like scraping aluminum, Dave Pennington fits three chords to some poem he wrote in study hall. When I hear his Honda 125 sputtering up the gravel drive like a bumblebee, I pull the guitar from the closet. His voice is weak, but put that cheap guitar in his lap, let him strum those same three chords and sing that heartache Buck Owens sang ten times better thirty years ago, you get something as real as sunshine. He's off to college soon. He asked me, "What should I major in?" I thought he might make a good teacher. "Takes one to know one," he said. Then he made up some funny hillbilly song and called it that, but we eventually twisted it into "Tastes One to Know One," then the party began.

Petey Pazillo is a little box shaped Italian guy who loves to massage me. Usually, it's the other way around, guys rolling over wanting me to rub their backs. Not Petey. He cracks his knuckles then slides his thick fingers into my neck and back and butt and calves…I'm getting drowsy just telling you about it. His hands are rough from construction work. If ever a man took the wrong road at the fork, it's Petey Pazillo. Put some lotion on those hands, send him to New York and he could make a mint on rich old ladies. But he could never leave Zoalmont because he's the fire chief and no one around here could best him there either.

Then there's Oliver Strange, who thinks everyone else in the world is strange. He's got his Master's in Biology but after teaching a few years in Arizona, he moved back and now builds silos with his uncles Moe and David. We flip through magazines and watch TV and he just mocks everyone in that dry way of his. During one Oliver visit I laughed so loud that Lizzy Sacksteder in the lot next door rapped on my door. This made me laugh all the harder and I told Oliver I felt like I was being shushed in church. When he heard the word "church" he did his hilarious bit proving the theory of evolution by comparing Catholics to carps. I wish I could repeat it, but I can never remember how it goes, but I still laugh like hell when he's saying it.

Dixie Walker says I have the body of a Roman statue. He likes to sketch me in the nude. By that I mean, I'm the one without the clothes on. "As long as you don't hang it up in your office," I told him and he laughed and said, "Maybe I'll sell more insurance that way."

And there's Harry Graves, who wanders off behind the trailer into the walnut grove and stares at the sky. He's shown me the bear, the hunter, the big and little dipper. Sometimes when I'm alone and need the bigness of the sky to feel a little humility, I try to find them but I can't. Once I thought I found the big dipper, but I couldn't zero in on the North Star. I felt empty and lost, so I checked my appointment book and saw that Harry was due in that week for a haircut and that was like finding my way back home.

There's Curtis Mifflin, whose wife ran off with his cousin and left him with those two darling brown-eyed daughters. Like the rest of us, he needs company now and again.

Milo Markko taught me how to play backgammon.

Frank Dwyler doesn't have much to say, but he's got a good eye and noticed my wallpaper bubbling up in the corner by the stove and spent half a Sunday redoing it for me.

Kenny Frazier doesn't come out anymore because he found Jesus, but he still keeps his standing appointment with me at Willa's and seeing his smile in the mirror when I brush off his shoulders still lights up my day.

August Finnegan has such a beautiful deep voice that I told him he could be a radio newscaster if he didn't have the most uncitizen-like attitude about politics.

Bobby Bosella is one of just three guys in the entire U.S. Army whose job it was to bring the mail in at Jimmy Carter's peanut farm.

And Cecil Finch is the only one I encourage to spend the night because he makes the best pancakes for breakfast. He won't tell me the special ingredients though he assures me they're right here in my own kitchen.

Then there's that what's-his-name Quinn who drives around the state shooting school portraits at schools. He keeps saying he'll shoot mine, but he never gets that camera out of the car.

And now I hear those owls and I think of Spooky Perry, who got me to take a twilight hike off the park property through the thickets. "Listen to them whispering pines," he said. And he led me to the hilltop where we could watch the town turn off its lights one by one. He said, "Can you see the railroad tracks. They stretch eight miles into Franklinville." It was dark out and I couldn't see the tracks, but Spooky knew that Amtrak rolled through town at 2:47 every morning. He lit a match and looked at his watch. Then he pointed to a dot of light miles away and we watched it get bigger and closer.

"The lonely eye of the night," he said.

"All those people on board," I said.

"Heading east," he said.

"Wonder if it's easy to sleep on a train," I said.

"If you can't sleep, you make love," said Spooky. "I'm not the least bit sleepy right now, are you?"

"No," I said, "and if it weren't for all these mosquitoes…"

We laughed and watched the train roll on to bigger things, but nothing better. There's nothing better than that moment.

These are all good people. But there are bad ones, too, who don't know what goes on inside my four walls. They see bikes and cars and trucks parked outside and they think I'm cheap. What they don't know about me could fill a lake.

I'll be downtown having a beer with Susie Rienzi and Patty Clackton and the dudes will strut by, cocky as Clydesdales and one of them will say something like, "You're all lookin' sweet tonight. Been doing aerobics?" They make their eyes sparkle, but all I see in those eyes is fear or dumb.

They offer to buy us a drink, like Don Corleone, making an offer we can't refuse. But when I do, they say, "You ain't shit, Sherri. Maybe I oughta take a number and wait in line."

I love Zoalmont. It's beautiful country. Quiet streets and old houses, and when the sidewalks end, farms begin. Honest people and fresh air. No McDonald's, thank God. Not yet. And no more than an hour or two in four directions from cities with skylines and big league teams.

Now, God help me get my home back.

Two weeks ago I was relaxing, washing my hair – imagine me going to work with dull hair – and listening to music. I had suds in my eyes. My head was underwater. I couldn't hear much except that my stereo in the living room suddenly got louder.

I squinted through the suds. There was Vinnie Bernadina in his oily clothes swinging around a half empty jug of red wine. "Mom said never come empty handed, so I brought you a present," he said, swishing the bottle at me.

"Ever hear of knocking?"

"Knock-knock," he said.

"People usually knock on the outside of the door and wait to be asked in," I said. He stood there like a totem pole. He stank and needed a shave, but then, he'd stunk and needed a shave since 11th grade. "Vinnie, I can't party tonight," I said – like we'd ever even partied before, just the two of us – "I've got to open Willa's tomorrow."

Vinnie ignored me and pulled a book from my shelf. He held it awkwardly, like a bachelor with a baby. I didn't want trouble so I decided to just talk a little to loosen up the awkwardness. "What did you do, float out here? I didn't hear you pull up. You still driving that Dodge?"

"Yeah, Sherri, I am," he said from behind the book. "Yeah, I'm still driving that Dodge." He sounded weird, like a robot. He was sauced. His lips wrestled with his words.

"Well, you must've fixed the exhaust or I'd have heard you a mile away." Vinnie Bernadina returned the book upside down to the shelf, then fell a little drunk to the couch. His face hung forward making two extra chins on his patchy-haired face. His head rolled around and he squinted at the portraits on the wall.

"Hey, that's your sister Janice. She was two years ahead of us."

"Her name's Janine," I said.

"Ja-neeeeen…right. Are those her kids?"

He wasn't going to leave. He was just going to kill the wine and pass out. Of all nights, when I had to open early in the morning.

"Is that your parents?" He didn't care who it was. It could've been me and the Beatles on a picnic. He gulped from the bottle. Red wine dribbled down his chin and damn near stained my couch.

"Will you drink coffee if I make it?" I asked.

He didn't answer, just hummed to himself.

While I poured water into the electric percolator, the humming stopped. I turned and he was gone. Before I could even wonder what-the-hell, he was behind me. He grabbed my neck and shoulder. The coffee pot crashed to the floor. He went crazy and whacked me against the walls so hard the house rocked.

Since first grade, Vinnie Bernadina was nothing more to me than a smelly egg. I always liked his older brother, who was cute and smart and polite and had gone off and made something of himself. But Vinnie, he was trying to stuff me through my own bedroom door, like I was dirty jeans going down a laundry chute.

"Vinnie – Jesus Christ!"

"Okay," he said, suddenly afraid of himself. He stopped throwing me around but tightened his grip on my wrists.

"Vinnie, let's go look at the stars."

He ignored me and pulled me to the bed. I reached for the closet door.

"You want to play me something on the guitar?" I asked.

He gripped my shoulders and aimed me at the bed.

"You play backgammon?" I reached for the game box on my dresser.

More firmly, he pushed me onto the bed. My robe came open.

Then it was eerie. Calm and steady. His knuckles whitened while his grip was tight as handcuffs. A song echoed in my mind, Frank Sinatra singing "Nice and easy does it…nice and easy does it…nice and easy does it…" but the song was very woozy and scary. Vinnie's sweat dripped onto my face. It all lasted a minute. I could stretch out a sneeze longer than that.

Then Vinnie Bernadina ascended from me.

"Can you make pancakes?" I asked.

This puzzled him, then scared him, and he ran from the room.

"Can you show me the North Star?" I said without getting up.

Vinnie got to the door, then stepped back, grabbed his bottle of wine and hurried out. The door clapped behind him like a rifle shot. I grabbed a stack of magazines and called into the darkness. "Do you want to flip through some magazines? You want to watch some TV?"

He zigzagged to his truck, looking back over his shoulder a couple times.

"Want to climb to the hilltop?" I said through the bedroom window.

He revved his truck.

"It's a clear night, Vinnie. Maybe we could look at the stars! Maybe we could see the train."

The truck engine purred as it took off down the gravel road. I don't know what I was thinking, chasing him down the road. My robe was all untied. Rocks cut into my feet. I shouted, "Thanks for getting a new muffler for me, Vinnie!"

Lizzy Sacksteder flicked her lights on and off. "Get a muffler on your mouth, Sherri."

"Vinnie Bernadina got a new muffler for me," I sang to high heaven. Lizzy rushed over to me, half-mad, half-not-knowing-what. "Are you drunk, Sherri?"

Then Lizzie became alarmed. "What in the – Lord God, close your robe, sweetie."

I just collapsed and cried while old Lizzy Sacksteder sat down and held me. She's almost a foot shorter, with arthritis that just kills her, but she held me up like a mighty oak. Together, we limped back to my place. She washed my face, put pajamas on me. Put the tea kettle back on the stove. Boiled some water. Made some tea. Held the cup real gentle to my lips. "You'll be all right sweetie," she said. "Take a little sip. I put some honey in it."

I couldn't open the next morning. I didn't even make it to work. My face was bruised. My lips all swelled up. I had to take a vacation day.

Some vacation. A real vacation is when you're excited about someplace new. You're not quite sure what, but you have an idea, and you know – you just know – it's going to be good. I always tingled in anticipation of what might surprise me. I loved the not knowing, the skipping down the yellow brick road. But now I can't even see the road. The path is dark, except for the eyes of the owls on you at every turn.

Vikings

We had just finished Lamaze class number one and my husband, who had been inspired by the nurse to be good to me, carried the blanket and all the pillows to the car.

"Look," he said, pointing to the car parked next to us. "There's that other couple." It was the long haired guy with the pointy nose. He had asked the nurse, "Smoking's really bad for the baby, ain't it?"

"Of course," the nurse agreed. But there was something more to the long haired guy's story. "I have a four-year-old who is kinda autistic," he said. "His mother smoked during pregnancy. She drank, too. I think that was part of the cause. I kinda blame her."

"Did you smoke, too?" asked the nurse.

"Yeah," the long-haired guy said. "But I always tried going into another room."

The nurse bit her lip then told us the dangers of second-hand smoke and how a mother may as well shove the baby's face in front of the exhaust pipe of a car. "That's a pretty effective way of saying it," the long-haired guy said with an awkward laugh.

My husband and I rolled our eyes. "We're classmates with Cheech and Chong," he said. Ever since I started to show, we began for the first time to feel like parents. But not until now did we feel like parents in the world of other parents. My husband whispered, "Their kid will probably want to date ours. He and I will be the dads in the wedding picture."

"Those two aren't married," I said, meaning the long-haired guy and the pregnant girl with him. "They're kinda married, like that kid's kinda autistic, like he kinda blames her." The nurse paused from her lecture and looked our way, so I shut up. I was done talking.

My husband touched my shoulder and I trembled. For the first time, I was afraid of the dangers my child would face, threats that I would have no power to deflect. The chasm that separates ignorance from wisdom and haphazard indifference from protective love had been bridged by a powerful horde of invading Vikings. Brutish, trampling, swath cutting barbarians at our gate.

It was bitterly cold outside. Our two cars were sealed up with tight windows and blasting heat. The long-haired guy in the driver's seat leaned over his woman, gave us a wide grin. A lit cigarette bobbed from his lips and he gave us the thumbs up sign.

I felt a kick from the life inside me. It was a protest.

Mark Morelli is also the author of *Effwords: Faith, Family, Fatherhood & That Other One*, wrote and published the humor 'zine *PAH!* from 1988-2008, and contributed the column "Rearview" to the web magazine *Halfsquare* from 2005-2008. He has been a college teacher, copywriter, reporter, deejay, wedding officiant and quiz game writer. He is still a daily visitor to the melancholy fringe.

Find other books, articles & writing at
www.markmorelli.net